A King Production presents…

Keep The Family Close...

A Novel

Joy Deja King

This novel is a work of fiction. Any references to real people, events, establishments, or locales are intended only to give the fiction a sense of reality and authenticity. Other names, characters, and incidents occurring in the work are either the product of the author's imagination or are used fictitiously, as those fictionalized events and incidents that involve real persons. Any character that happens to share the name of a person who is an acquaintance of the author, past or present, is purely coincidental and is in no way intended to be an actual account involving that person.

Cover concept by Joy Deja King
Cover Model: Joy Deja King

Graphic design: www.anitaart79.wixsite.com/bookdesign
Typesetting: www. anitaart79.wixsite.com/anita

Library of Congress Cataloging-in-Publication Data;
King, Deja Joy
The Legacy Part 3: a novel/by Joy Deja King

For complete Library of Congress Copyright info visit;
www.joydejaking.com Twitter: @joydejaking

A King Production
P.O. Box 912, Collierville, TN 38027

A King Production and the above portrayal logo are trademarks of A King Production LLC

Copyright © 2022 by Joy Deja King. All rights reserved. No part of this book may be reproduced in any form without the permission from the publisher, except by reviewer who may quote brief passage to be printed in a newspaper or magazine.

This Book is Dedicated To My:

Family, Readers, and Supporters. I LOVE you guys so much. Please believe that!!

A special THANK YOU to RG, for motivating me to get back to doing what I love. I will always adore you. For Life.

—Joy Deja King

The Legacy...

A Trilogy

"Each Betrayal Begins With Trust
Blood Makes You Related
Loyalty Makes You Family..."

A KING PRODUCTION

The Final Chapter

The Legacy Part III

Keep The Family Close...

A Novel

Joy Deja King

Chapter One

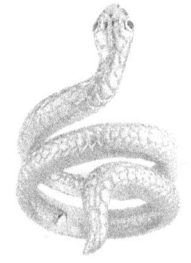

What You Won't Do For Love

A cloud of darkness filled Allen's deep-set, caramel-colored eyes. His dense, velvety brows furrowed with contempt at Caesar, who stood assertively, intent on muscling in on his space.

"I advise you to step back and leave my home while you're still standing," Allen warned, with flames flickering in his eyes, leading you into an endless stretch of midnight that would've chilled almost anyone else to the bone. But Caesar was unmoved. His desire to win back the woman he had fallen deeply in love with, gave Caesar a voracious appetite to destroy the man who was acting as an impasse to getting what he wanted most.

"I don't take advice from men who have their own daughter's kidnapped and then place the blame on another man," Caesar countered.

"You've crossed the line, now get the fuck out my house." This was no slow burn. Allen didn't attempt to keep his composure as he wanted Caesar to know he was enraged, and his life was in danger.

"I'm not going anywhere until…" Caesar paused when he noticed Karmen entering the foyer. Allen turned his head around to see what had caught Caesar's attention.

"Allen, are you joining me for dinner?" Karmen asked before stopping midway, when she noticed her former lover standing behind her husband. "Caesar, what are you doing here?"

"How do you know this man?" Allen questioned in an accusatory tone, pointing his finger at Caesar.

"Karmen, I'm glad you're here. There's something I need to tell you," Caesar said walking past Allen.

"Don't you dare go near my wife!" Allen fumed, seizing Caesar's arm. "I will break your fuckin' neck," he spit. Allen was much older than Caesar, but his body frame was solid. The man maintained his powerful physique with the same diligence he ran his lucrative business empire. So, although Caesar was physically fit, Allen had no qualms brawling with the younger man.

"Don't you ever put yo' muthafuckin' hands on me!" Caesar released his arm from Allen's grasp. They were standing nose to nose about to exchange blows.

"Stop!" Karmen screamed, racing over to stand between the two men. At that moment, Jackson came walking through the door, and without asking any questions, he pulled out his gun, sensing something was wrong.

"Jackson, I need you to get this intruder out my house before I'm forced to have you put a bullet in his head," Allen instructed.

"Of course, boss."

"Put that gun away. Now!" Karmen demanded. Jackson made eye contact with Allen, not willing to lower his weapon without a direct order from his boss. There seemed to be a prolonged delay before Allen responded to his wife's demand.

"I want this man out my house and then Jackson will put his gun away." That was the extent of Allen's compromising.

"I'm not leaving until I speak to Karmen," Caesar insisted.

"Just go...please," Karmen asserted, placing her hand on top of his. Her touch made Caesar weak, and he wanted to hold her in his arms.

"Man, you better listen to Mrs. Collins," Jackson nodded, with his gun on display.

Caesar stared at Karmen as her eyes pleaded with him to leave. He then glared over at Allen, whose superior demeanor incensed him. "This isn't over," he stated before making his exit.

"Jackson, make sure that piece of shit gets the hell off this property," Allen seethed, clenching his jaw.

Karmen watched as Jackson followed behind Caesar, shaking her head in dismay. "Are you ready to sit down for dinner?" she asked, wanting to move past what had just occurred.

"Not until you tell me how you know that man. He seemed enamored with you."

"You're being ridiculous. We're both members of that private gym that opened a few months ago. We've run into each other a few times and engaged in some casual conversations. He's definitely not enamored with me," Karmen said, doing her best to erase the idea from her husband's mind. "What did he want?"

"Nothing of importance. He was spewing lies, but he'll be dealt with. In the meantime, I want you to stay away from that man."

"What sort of lies?"

"Nothing you need to concern yourself with. Just stay away from him. As a matter of fact, cancel your membership at that gym. You can workout at the country club or have a personal trainer come here. Someone in this house needs to use that state-of-the-art gym I had built."

"Sure," Karmen agreed not wanting to raise Allen's

suspicions any further by seeming overly concerned by what transpired between the two men.

"Now we can eat," Allen said taking his wife's hand. While making their way to the formal dining room, dinner was the very last thing on Allen's mind. Instead, he wanted to find out everything he could about Caesar, while simultaneously plotting on how he would silence him permanently.

Zephan X Spotted At The Beach on an early morning walk with an unknown beauty...

Elesia read the headline on one of her favorite gossip blogs three times before reading the accompanying article. "Why does this chick look so familiar to me," she commented after Damacio stepped out the shower and came into the bedroom. He seemed preoccupied, and ignored what Elesia said as if he didn't hear her.

"Are you staying in bed all day or what?" he asked before disappearing into the sprawling walk-in closet to get dressed.

"Holy shit! I knew this chick looked fuckin' familiar. This is your ex-wife!" Elesia exclaimed. "I saw her downstairs when I came out the bedroom naked that time."

That announcement garnered Damacio's attention, who came storming back into the bedroom. "What the fuck did you just say?"

"Your ex-wife is dating Zephan X!" she broadcasted, holding up her iPhone.

"Ashton is not my ex-wife. We're still married." Damacio corrected Elesia as he grabbed her phone and started reading the article.

"Wait, so I'm dating the husband of the woman who is fucking with superstar rapper Zephan X. This is some bizarre shit."

"She must've met him at that rehab," Damacio blurted angrily. "Unfuckin' believable."

"But he announced on his Instagram he was taking a break due to exhaustion. Are you telling me he's actually been at a drug rehab?" she wanted all the details.

"I don't know what the fuck this Zephan dude is doing, but I've spoken to Ashton a few times and she's still at the rehab in Ventura, California."

Elesia prized herself on being a social media sleuth, so she scoured online pics to see what beach they were seen walking at. "Bingo, these pics were taken at a beach in Ventura. That's crazy your wife is dating Zephan X. He's like right up there with Drake. That must really sting, but at least you have me baby," Elesia smiled, gliding her lithe body across the bed, draping her arms around Damacio's back. "Your wife might be walking on the beach and holding hands with a super famous rapper, but she has to be missing this dick." Elesia slid her hand underneath the towel that was wrapped around his waist.

"Not right now, Elesia." Damacio tried to shrug her off, but her grip was strong on his dick and the hand job had his middle muscle hard. Before he could do any further protesting, she was down on her knees showcasing her impeccable deep throat skills. The images of Ashton with another man were consuming Damacio's thoughts but soon those images were replaced with watching Elesia's lips and tongue swathed around his hardened tool. He chose to welcome the escape and laid back on the bed with his legs firmly planted on the dove grey brushed limestone floor. But even with Elesia's exceptional head game, Damacio's mind continued to wander back to his wife.

Damn Ashton how did it come to this. It seems like yesterday we defied our families because we were madly in love. Now you're walking on the beach with another man, and my dick is down another woman's throat. I want to blame your addiction to drugs but maybe we just weren't meant to be, and our marriage was simply doomed from the start. I don't even fuckin' know anymore. Maybe my father is right, and it's time for me to let go, Damacio thought as he ejaculated in Elesia's mouth, releasing all of his frustration.

"I would offer you a drink, but under the circumstances I know that's a bad idea," Lizzie said pouring herself another glass of bubbly. "I can't believe I finished this bottle," she frowned, signaling for the waiter to bring over some more champagne.

"I really do appreciate you meeting me for lunch," Vannette said, nibbling on her Asian grilled chicken salad. "I know me spending the last hour whining to you about Clayton, wasn't exactly how you planned to spend your Saturday afternoon."

"True." Lizzie acknowledged. "But I know this is what Ashton would want. Since she's away at rehab and unable to be your sounding board, I promised her now that I'm no longer attending school in Boston and back in Houston, I would be here for you. I'm not really good at giving advice. That's more so Ashton's thing, but I'm a pretty good listener."

"Yeah, Ashton is great at giving advice. She's very no-nonsense with it but believe it or not, you listening to me is very therapeutic."

"Well, I'm glad to know that. I mean I can listen to you all day as long as the champagne keeps flowing," Lizzie giggled. "But seriously, I will say this. You're in the early stages of your pregnancy. I don't think it's a good idea to be stressing yourself out."

"I know but what can I do?"

"Maybe you should stay away from your baby daddy for a minute, since he's the source of your stress," Lizzie suggested, taking another sip of her champagne.

"Clayton isn't the prime source of my stress, it's Brianna."

"Brianna..." Lizzie paused for a moment as if getting her thoughts together. "That's the other woman who is pregnant with his child...correct?"

"Correct," Vannette nodded.

"She was also your good friend from New York?"

"Yep," Vannette continued to nod. "You really are a good listener."

"I try to be. I'll admit this is a complicated situation," Lizzie conceded, shaking her head. "I'm still a tad shocked notorious Playboy Clayton has two women that used to be good friends, pregnant at the same time. If it wasn't for the fact that I know you personally, this might be somewhat amusing. But because we're cool and I see how distraught you are, it's pretty tragic."

"I know but I don't know what to do. When I first told Clayton I was pregnant, we were about to plan our wedding. Then that bitch Brianna showed up announcing she was pregnant too. I didn't even have ten minutes to celebrate being engaged to the man of my dreams," Vannette sobbed.

"Please don't cry," Lizzie pleaded, putting down her glass.

"Dammit, I wish Ashton was here. She would know what to say to make you feel better."

Consequently, within a matter of seconds, things went from bad to worse. As Lizzie was trying to console an overwrought Vannette, the man of the hour walked in the restaurant hand in hand with her rival.

"I'm going to kill that bitch!" Vannette snapped, clutching the knife on the table.

Lizzie glanced up go to see what had Vannette going from distraught to full blown rage. Right away she noticed Clayton walking towards a corner booth with a young lady. "Let me guess, that's Brianna."

"You damn right! Since they ruined my lunch, I'm going to ruin theirs." Vannette threw her napkin down on the table and stormed off.

"Vannette wait!" Lizzie called out but of course she was ignored. "Fuck! What would Ashton do?" she mumbled, gulping down the last of her champagne before chasing after Vannette. Lizzie was not a relationship expert or a therapist, but she recognized Vannette, Clayton and Brianna were on a collision course that could lead to catastrophic repercussions.

Chapter Two

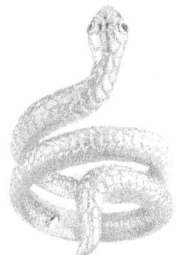

Russian Roulette

"That nigga gonna die, but before he does, I'ma take everything away from him, starting with his wife," Caesar swore.

"Yo, you need to calm down," Darius advised, letting out a deep sigh. "I warned you this would be all bad if you got involved with that man's wife."

"Fuck Allen Collins! He don't deserve Karmen."

"It don't matter what you think that man deserve. That's his wife. You 'bout to go to war over a woman that don't even belong to you."

"Karmen would be mine if she knew the truth. She was ready to walk away from her marriage and be with me, but she's worried about her kids, especially Ashton." Caesar wanted to be unemotional but he yearned for the woman he had fallen in love with.

"You mean their kids," Darius reminded Caesar. "I love you like a brother, so I'ma always keep it one hundred wit' you. She didn't leave her marriage. She over there wit' her husband, living like a queen at that fuckin' humongous estate. This ain't you Caesar. You willing to give it all up for some designer pussy?"

"Fuck you, Darius. This ain't about sex. She's the one…the only one for me. When Karmen finds out that the man she's married to, had his own daughter kidnapped, their marriage is over. Ashton was traumatized behind that bullshit. To the point she got strung out on drugs to numb the pain and now she's in rehab."

"Listen, I get all that. It's some foul shit what that nigga did. But it's *his* family. That's *they* business, stay the fuck out of it."

"I can't do that," Caesar shook his head. "Once I fell in love with Karmen, she became my business."

"We makin' so much money. You ready to fuck that up? I hope this woman worth you playing Russian roulette, because if you don't let this shit go, it's gonna get deadly."

"The only person that's gonna die is Allen Collins. You right though," Caesar said turning around to face Darius. "Things will get deadly, so I need to know are you all in? If not, my love for you won't change, but I'ma need you to step out the way."

"I don't approve of this shit, but we been locked in since elementary school, so I'm forever all in." Darius stated without hesitation.

"Then let's get this done. The sooner I put an end to Allen Collins, the sooner we're fully back to business," Caesar surmised.

"Can I help you?" Kasir asked the woman who was standing in the entryway of his office. "Are you lost?"

"Sorry for just poppin' up like this but there wasn't anyone out front."

"My assistant is on her lunch break. Pretty much everyone on the top floor is out for lunch. Did you have an appointment with someone here?" Kasir asked, confused by the presence of this unknown woman.

"I guess you don't remember me. I'm Crystal's friend, Remi. We met that first night at the restaurant with Lance."

"Oh yes! Come in, have seat," Kasir said, quickly warming up to Remi, wanting to accommodate her. "How is Crystal? I've been trying to get in touch with her for months but she pretty much disappeared."

"That's why I'm here," Remi said nervously, sitting down.

"Wait, you haven't heard from Crystal either?" he questioned becoming alarmed.

"Not in a few weeks. Last time I talked to her, we were linking up to go to this concert. I was running late but she never showed up. I was calling, but she didn't answer. At first, I thought maybe she was pissed at me because I was so late but then the next day, I still couldn't get her on the phone. I stopped by her apartment, and she hasn't been there. I even went to the police department to file a missing person report. Them muthafuckas didn't take me seriously though. They wrote down the information but there's been no follow-up. I'm desperate. Please help me find my friend," Remi pleaded.

"I'm not sure what you want me to do," Kasir said trying to process what he just learned. "You and Crystal are obviously close, so you should know that we haven't been in contact. For whatever reason, she cut me off. So again, I'm not sure what I can do to help."

"I know you cared about her at one time…"

"I still do," Kasir said, interrupting Remi.

"You have money and resources that gives you plenty of access to find my best friend."

"Are you sure Crystal wants to be found? Maybe it's a reason she disappeared. Perhaps she ran off with that married man she was seeing,"

Kasir noticed Remi shifting in her chair. Her eyes darted in every direction around the room but his. He knew he struck a nerve and hoped if he pushed a bit harder, she would share the information that only a best friend would know.

"I think it was a bad idea coming here." Remi stood up fidgeting with her purse, not wanting to leave but also feeling it was a bad idea to stay.

"If you want my help, then you have to be honest with me Remi. I can't bring Crystal back home if I don't know why she might've vanished in the first place."

When Remi sat back down in the chair, Kasir knew she was ready to talk. He walked over to close his office door and lock it. He didn't want them to be interrupted. He had a strong sentiment, that whatever Remi revealed would be consequential.

"Isn't this cute. My former friend and the father of my child having lunch together." Vannette was breathing heavy with her arms folded tightly hovering over them as they sat in the booth.

"I am pregnant. It's important that I eat. You know for my health and our baby," Brianna taunted, placing her hand on Clayton's upper leg.

"You bitch! I'm pregnant too!" Vannette barked.

"Vannette, keep your voice down," Clayton demanded in a low but stern tone.

"Why, am I embarrassing you?" she shouted with defiance.

"Sit down!" Clayton stood and smiled at the few people who had turned in their direction, to see what the commotion was. "Sit down now," he seethed under his breath placing his arm on Vannette's wrist, in an attempt to force her to sit down in the chair.

"Fine!" she agreed, as her breathing remained elevated.

"Can you please bring her a glass of water, immediately," Clayton told a waitress who was walking by. "Vannette, you need to calm down. Getting worked up can't be good for the baby."

"As if you care," she scoffed.

"Of course, I care," Clayton leaned forward and told her. "That's my child you're carrying."

"I'm surprised you remember."

"Please don't be upset." Clayton picked up his napkin and dabbed a tear trickling down Vannette's cheek. "Why don't you join us for lunch," he suggested.

"Babe, I don't..." Before Brianna could continue, Clayton cut her off.

"We would like that, right Brianna?"

"Of course," she lied.

"I can't. I'm actually here with Lizzie," Vannette said, noticing her lurking at a nearby table.

"Lizzie, she went to school with Ashton," Clayton said, recognizing his sister's best friend from high school. "I see Lizzie still loves the bubbly," he joked. "She can join us too."

"That's okay. I've lost my appetite." Vannette stood

up.

"Then don't let us keep you. You should go," Brianna remarked, her voice dripping with annoyance.

"You're such a bitch!" Vannette spit. "I know you wish you could get rid of me, and you were the only one carrying Clayton's child, but I'm having his baby too."

"We know, and so does everyone else in this restaurant. You keep reminding us over and over again." Brianna rolled her eyes in disgust.

"The two of you need to stop...now!" Clayton commanded. "Both of you are carrying my child, so I suggest you learn to get along."

"You expect me to get along with that snake. She was supposed to be my friend, but instead she plotted to get in your bed."

"The way I remember things, I was invited in his bed. Isn't that right?" Brianna turned to Clayton, provoking Vannette.

"You're about to be a mother, both of you," Clayton shook his head, giving the women grimacing stares. "It's time to grow the fuck up," he scolded, leaving them both at the table.

"Look what you did. All your nagging made Clayton walk off," Brianna complained, glancing down at her French manicure.

"Vannette, are you ready to go?" Lizzie came over and asked, seeing things were about to erupt between her and Brianna.

"I will be in one moment." Vannette scooted in the

booth next to Brianna.

"What are you doing...move!" Brianna tried to put some space between her former friend.

"You can move away from me all you want," Vannette snarled with a wild, crazy glare in her eyes. "You might think because you're pregnant, all your money dreams are about to come true. But I actually love Clayton, and I promise, you will never have him."

"I promise you, that I will." Brianna stated confidently, tossing her hair behind her bare shoulder.

"I'll see you dead first before that ever happens," Vannette threatened with a wicked smile, leaving Brianna spooked.

"What did you say to her?" Lizzie sought answers. "All the color drained from her face, and she appears frozen."

"Nothing she didn't already know. That Clayton belongs with me and anyone who tries to come between us will suffer the consequences. Surely Brianna wouldn't risk losing her life over a man that doesn't belong to her."

Lizzie decided to blame it on the alcohol, as she did finish up two bottles of champagne, which had her extremely tipsy. She preferred to believe her buzz made her slightly incoherent and she didn't hear Vannette correctly. Because Lizzie refused to believe that ultrasensitive Vannette had turned into a certifiable nut.

Chapter Three

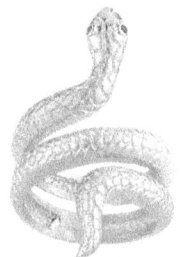

California Breeze

Behind the privacy enhancing gates, the Malibu blufftop estate made for a serene escape. The crash of the ocean waves lapping the shore created a harmonious calmness. The endless sunsets and natural white noise relaxed the mind, suppressing the inessential clamors, forming a tranquil ambiance. The soothing sound of waves on the beach made for the perfect backdrop for the newly enchanted lovers.

"Have I told you how much I love fuckin' you," Zephan said after Ashton slid off his dick and laid back in the bed next to him.

"Yeah, you pretty much tell me every time we have sex," she smiled reaching for a cigarette off the nightstand.

"Pass me one too," Zephan said sitting up in the bed and turning on the television.

"I really need to kick this nicotine habit but it's better I reach for a cigarette than some coke," Ashton reasoned.

"You ain't thought about gettin' one more hit since we been here?" Zephan questioned inhaling the cigarette smoke.

"Every freakin' day," she admitted. "But I will say, the counseling I've been getting since we've been in rehab has seriously helped. Instead of reaching for pills or coke, I'm finding more productive ways to cope with the pain. You know like when we take those walks together on the beach," Ashton beamed, leaning over kissing Zephan on his chiseled chocolate chest.

"You 'bout to get my dick hard again," he mumbled, playing in Ashton's hair. "Yo, speakin' of beaches, the paparazzi got footage of us holding hands, walking on the beach. This shit crazy!" he laughed, watching the commentary on an entertainment and celebrity news show. "Baby girl you famous," Zephan cracked.

Ashton turned to look at the television and was stunned to see her face plastered on the screen. For now, the show was referring to her as some unknown beauty, but she knew that would soon change. The media would start digging until they got a name.

"I can't believe this shit!" Ashton became panicked.

"It's all good. I want the world to see my new baby girl. It's nice to have some fresh pussy that ain't nobody in the industry ran through," Zephan boasted.

"You don't understand," she said nervously. "I've been here in California with you cut off from the world but there's a whole other life in Houston waiting for me."

"I like Houston. I got a lot of fans out there. We can stop through and visit your fam," he assured Ashton.

"I'm not sure my family would approve of you but then again, I guess my father would prefer you over my husband."

"WTF, you married?!" Zephan's chill demeanor promptly turned cold. "You neva told me you got a husband, and you ain't wearin' no wedding ring."

"It's complicated."

"Fuck complicated. I thought you was mine. I ain't into no sharing shit."

"You're not sharing me; my marriage is over. That's why I'm not wearing my wedding ring," Ashton said, starring down at her hand. She briefly thought about the exquisite diamond that used to adorn her finger.

"So, what, ya separated? I need answers. Your face all up on the television screen wit' me. You can't have me out here lookin' like a clown."

"Yeah, we're separated. But I wouldn't want him to

find out about us through the media, and certainly not my family."

"I guess it's time to make our relationship official," Zephan shrugged. "We can head to Houston and announce that shit to your fam and ex. Get it over wit'. 'Cause like I said, I ain't into that sharing shit."

"I hear you, but I doubt the rehab facility would want us leaving to take a trip so soon."

"They be letting us leave to come stay at my crib in Malibu," Zephan reminded her.

"That's only because they show you special treatment, plus it's only for the day. We would be gone for at least a few days."

"Don't worry about rehab, I'll handle that. You just make sure to let your family know we're coming home," Zephan asserted.

Ashton briefly scanned the generous oceanfront primary suite, before getting out of bed and stepping on the French white oak wide plank floor. She followed the panorama of whitewater ocean to the glass doors leading out on the terrace. She needed a moment alone to gather her thoughts. She struggled with the idea of announcing to her family that she had moved on with a new man, especially since she still loved Damacio. Ashton couldn't decide if their relationship was predestined to end in heartache or if she needed to fight harder for her marriage.

"Do you have a phone I can use?" Ashton asked Zephan, since she wasn't allowed to have her personal phone at rehab. The facility only permitted patients to make calls once a day from a landline.

"Yeah, why you about to call your fam and let them know we coming?" he questioned, handing Ashton one of his cell phones.

"Yep," she lied, heading back outside, closing the doors to the terrace as she called Damacio.

The phone rang four times before a female voice answered. "Hello."

"Who is this?" Ashton wanted to know, thinking that maybe she dialed the wrong number.

"This is Elesia. Who is this?"

"I must have the wrong number," she said about to hang up.

"Are you calling for Damacio?"

"Yes I am."

"He just got out the shower. I'll go get him. Who should I say is calling?"

"Ashton." *Calm down Ashton, don't overreact. It's probably nothing. Don't start cursing the woman out. Before you go off, wait and speak to Damacio. Take a deep breath and count backwards from ten to one,* she told herself. She was determined to utilize some of the de-escalation exercises she'd learned during her stint at rehab, because the calmative California breeze wasn't working

"Hi, what can I do for you?" Damacio's indifferent tone did little to calm Ashton's nerves.

"Who answered your phone?"

"A friend of mine."

"What friend?"

"I think you met her once at the house, the day before you left for rehab."

"You mean the naked woman who came out of our bedroom, that friend?"

"Yep, that would be her."

"Oh, so she wasn't a one and done, you're still seeing her. Is she like your girlfriend?"

"That's none of your business."

"What do you mean it's none of my business?! Last I checked, I'm still your wife!"

"Really, because you didn't seem concerned about being a wife when you were holding hands with another man."

"What are you talking about, Damacio?"

"I saw the pictures of you walking on the beach holding hands with another man, Ashton. So, you can stop with the bullshit."

"It's not what you think..."

"Then what is it?" Damacio asked cutting her off. "You know what, don't answer that question because it doesn't matter."

"It does matter. I want to explain."

"I don't want to hear it!" he barked. "Clearly we've both moved on, so save your explanations."

"But Damacio...Damacio," Ashton called out a few times before realizing he was no longer on the line. "He fuckin' hung up on me!" she seethed ready to throw the phone in the ocean. But instead of tossing the phone into the deep blue sea, Ashton placed another call. "Hey daddy. I just wanted to let you know, I'm on my way home.

Chapter Four

Tread Carefully

Gustaf waited in Caesar's office staring out the glass panel at the four men in the vast warehouse. They were standing over the table examining the extensive artillery. Each holding a semi-automatic with a detachable magazine, a pistol grip and a vertical forward grip, flash suppressor, or barrel shroud. They were dressed in army fatigue as if preparing for war.

"I apologize for keeping you waiting but I had to handle something," Caesar said closing the office door.

"Not a problem. Alejo explain you a very busy man.

He tell me to work around your schedule," Gustaf said, in his thick Spanish accent continuing to watch how the men in the warehouse navigated.

"I appreciate Alejo accommodating my schedule, but I'm invested in getting this done also. My men are prepared to make their move."

"Are those the men you speak of?" he asked, nodding his head towards the four killers in army fatigue.

"Yeah, that's the crew I put together. They my best shooters. Not one of them will miss their target," Caesar spoke confidently.

"We only have a single target, correct?"

Caesar raised an eyebrow. "Why do you ask me that?"

"Alex Collins is one man, but your crew look prepared to take out a small village."

Caesar released a heavy chuckle. "I guess I wanna be overly prepared. We don't want the same results as you got before, so I'm just putting glue on both sides of the ball to make sure we don't fumble."

"I respect that," Gustaf nodded. "We can't have any missteps this time. Alejo won't be as forgiving towards me."

"No worries. I can guarantee my men will deliver. Allen Collins is good as dead. All you have to do is let me know when you ready to infiltrate his location."

"I must say, I'm sensing you anxious for Mr. Collins to meet his demise," Gustaf remarked. "Would I be correct with my assessment?"

"You would be," Caesar acknowledged.

"Might I ask why?"

"Let's just say he has something that I want."

"And you need him dead to get it?"

"I do have another option but having him dead would make things a lot easier and less complicated. So, when do you want my men to get this done?"

"Alejo wants it to happen on the first."

"That's not for another two weeks. Why the delay? I was under the impression Alejo was eager to get this handled."

"He is but Alejo wants something else to unfold before getting rid of Mr. Collins."

"Unfold...what would that be?" Caesar wanted to know.

"Honestly, I'm not sure. Initially he wanted this resolved immediately, but on my way here to see you, things changed. Unfortunately, I don't have any further details to give you. Alejo is the boss, so I move when he says move."

"I get that," Caesar said becoming distracted by a text message coming through.

"Now that I'm aware you have your own reasons for wanting Allen Collins dead, I get you might be disappointed with waiting, but it's only a couple weeks," Gustaf pointed out. "Alejo assured me his intent hasn't changed. He wants Mr. Collins dead."

"I understand. I'll let my men know, but um I have another matter that needs to be dealt with. I'm sure you can see your way out," he told Gustaf. Caesar abruptly left out his office to exit the warehouse, signaling his men to follow suit.

"Clayton, it's so good to see you," Karmen smiled warmly, hugging her youngest son.

"I'm happy to see you too. I really miss you." Clayton welcomed his mother's embrace, holding her close. "Recently it seems we haven't had much time to spend with each other," he said taking a seat on the handcrafted statement high-back wing chair.

"Our family has been dealing with one crisis after another but regardless of that, we have to make quality time for each other. The moment you told me you were stopping by, I had Bernice fix your favorite meal for lunch," Karmen beamed.

"There is nothing like one of Bernice's meals. That's one of the things I miss about living here."

"You're always welcome to move back home. This house feels like an empty museum now that you all have moved out."

"It won't feel so empty in the coming months," Clayton stated with consideration with how he should share the news with his mother.

"Wait, are you actually planning on moving back home?" Karmen leaned forward with excitement.

"Not exactly."

"Then what?"

"I'm going to be a father...of two."

Karmen placed her herbal tea down on the Pavolion martini table. "You're having twins?"

"No, I have two different women pregnant," he admitted, putting his head down. "I know this is not what you wanted and neither did I but..."

"But nothing, Clayton. I'm looking forward to being a grandmother. Those babies will be loved, so they are a blessing," his mother smiled.

"You're not upset with me? I turned away because I didn't want to see the disappointment on your face."

"Do you see a trace of disappointment," Karmen said pointing her finger at her cheerful expression. "I'm more concerned about you. You stated this is not what you wanted, so how did it happen? I mean I know how it happened," she laughed wanting to put her son at ease.

"I always use protection, trying to be cautious but things happen. I slipped up." Clayton owned up to his mistakes, taking full responsibility for the predicament he found himself in.

"Do I know either of the women?"

"Obviously, you know Vannette."

"I didn't realize the two of you were serious, but you have been seeing Vannette for a while now. There is history, which is good."

"At first, I felt the same way until I found out Brianna, the other woman I had been seeing was also pregnant. That makes things a lot more complicated. I want to be there for both my kids equally."

"And you can be."

"The thing is, when Vannette first told me she was pregnant, I told her we would get married. When I found out Brianna was also pregnant, I changed my mind."

"You must have feelings for Brianna."

"I do," Clayton conceded. "We haven't known each other long but things flow easy with her. Vannette on the other hand is," he paused releasing a heavy sigh.

"She's what?"

"Angry."

"Does she have reason to be?"

Before Clayton could respond to his mother's question, his brother came charging into the room demanding answers to his own questions.

"Where is our father...is he here...if not when will he be home?" Kasir railed.

"Son, you're obviously upset." Karmen got up from her chair and walked over to her son. "What has you this agitated?" when she placed her hand on Kasir's shoulder he flinched.

"Is something going on with business?" Clayton was also now standing. "You seem off."

"This has nothing to do with business. I want to speak with our father."

"About what?"

"Clayton, mind your business. This has nothing to do with you," Kasir chided.

"Man, you need to calm down."

"The only thing I need, is to speak with our father. Do you know where he is or not?"

"Son, come sit down," Karmen urged. "Whatever has you this upset, we can fix it."

"Mother, this can't be fixed."

"We're family," Karmen said taking her son's hand. "There's nothing we can't fix."

"If you really want to fix this, tell me where Crystal is?"

"Why would you be asking our mother about Crystal?" Clayton could see his mother attempting to appear unfazed by Kasir's question and decided to intervene.

"Kasir, I'm not..."

"Just stop!" he exclaimed, preventing his mother from finishing her sentence. "I'm not interested in your denials or lies."

"Don't you disrespect our mother like that!' Clayton shouted.

"Let me handle this," Karmen held up her hand, signaling her youngest son to fall back.

"I have no idea where Crystal is and that's the truth. The first and only time we spoke, she said she was leaving but didn't tell me where she was going, and I didn't ask."

"What did you all speak about?"

"I asked her to stay away from you, but I'm assuming you're already aware of this."

"So, it's true, you did pay Crystal off?" Kasir was

irate even though Remi had already fed him the information. "When I was in the hospital, you already knew you cut her a check and she was gone. Instead of telling me the truth, you pretended to be concerned."

"I was concerned. I was trying to protect you Kasir," she implored.

"No, you were trying to protect our father!" his frustration boiling over. "Speaking of our father, look who finally showed up." Kasir stomped in his direction in full blown rage.

"What type of man are you! You were cheating on our mother with Crystal! And I'm just about positive it was your idea to have mother clean up your mess and pay her to disappear." Kasir was fired up, but Allen kept his composure.

"Kasir, that's not true. Your Father had no idea I planned on paying Crystal off."

"Why are you defending this man! He cheated on you repeatedly and didn't even have the balls to tell his own son they were having sex with the same woman! You disgust me," Kasir spit with disdain.

"You better watch your mouth!" Allen pointed his finger towards his son. "I'm your father and you damn sure not about to disrespect me in my own muthafuckin' home," he scolded.

"This isn't a home. A home is built off love not a bunch of lies," Kasir contended. "I came to you, begging for your help to locate Crystal because she'd vanished. You promised to have Vincent look into it. But it was all lies. What else have you been lying about father?"

Kasir's question sounded ominous to everyone standing in the room. There was too much deception hovering, waiting in the shadows to be revealed. No one said a word, as if contemplating not if their lies would be exposed but when.

"We need to take a step back and relax," Clayton proposed. "I understand you had feelings for her, but is this Crystal woman worth bringing chaos into our family?"

"Your brother is right," Karmen chimed in. "No matter how disappointed you are with your father's decisions, you knew Crystal had been seeing a married man. You admitted to me that you could not trust a woman like that. I understand you don't agree with me paying her off, but I could not take the chance of her hurting you. You're my son, and I will always do anything to protect you, Clayton and Ashton."

"I'm not a child and you should've been honest with me, but I recognize you were in a difficult position," Kasir conceded. "But you," he turned to his father. "I'm not sure if I can trust anything you say."

"Yes, I did make a horrible mistake cheating on your mother, but that's between me and my wife and we're committed to rebuilding the trust in our marriage. But Kasir, I had no idea you were seeing Crystal until she showed up at the hospital after you were shot and that's the truth," Allen proclaimed.

"Since you're in the mood to tell the truth, then

answer me this. Do you know what happened to Crystal?"

"No, I do not. I stopped seeing her months ago. The last time I spoke with Crystal was when she came to see you at the hospital," Allen insisted doubling down on his lie.

"Mother, what about you?"

"No. Like I told you earlier, I wrote her a check with one condition, for her to stay away from you. The only reason I knew she kept up her end of the agreement, is because you said you had been unable to get in contact with her."

"Kasir, the woman took the money and disappeared. Why are you so pressed to find her? She chose to take the check and walk away, so who cares where she is," Clayton denounced.

"I care because I believe something happened to her," Kasir told them.

"Something like what?" Karmen appeared confused.

"Her friend came to see me and said she was meeting up with Crystal at a concert and she never showed up. She went to her apartment and there's no sign of her. She hasn't only disappeared from my life; she has completely vanished without a trace," Kasir explained.

"Son, I get you're concerned but I think it's unwarranted. Maybe Crystal decided to cut ties with the city of Houston and left town, and she didn't have the heart to tell her friend. Whatever the reason, I'm sure she's fine and there's no need for you to worry. It's time for you to move on with your life and put Crystal behind you," Allen advised.

He stared deep into his father's eyes, searching to see if there was any trace of truth coming out his mouth. "I'm going to give you the benefit of the doubt and believe you're genuine. But if I find out that you're lying to me again, and you had anything to do with Crystal's disappearance, it won't end well for you," Kasir warned.

Chapter Five

Bloody Night

"Man, I should be there shortly. I'm right over here on Berry Road. I have to make one more stop up the street and then I'll be there," Jeff told Darius as he was leaving a convenience store in the 500 block of Berry Road in North Houston, walking towards his car in the parking lot.

"Cool, I'll see you when you get here," Darius said ending the call.

"Where is that fuckin' key," Jeff mumbled out loud digging in the front pocket of his jeans. Because he was distracted, he didn't see the white truck slowly driving behind him and the men lurking nearby. Within a matter of seconds, he was snatched up right off the street by three goons. Working in unanimity, the goons had Jeff tied up, blind folded and his hands were bound with a heavy-duty extension cord by the time they slammed the back door to the truck.

Once bundled in the truck they drove Jeff to a nearby house of a drug addict woman, who had no problem allowing the men to use her home as a torture chamber as long as she was compensated with crystal meth and a pipe to smoke it. For the next few hours, Jeff was imprisoned at the woman's house while a gang of at least six men tortured and assaulted him.

"Where you keep your drugs and money?" one of the men demanded to know. "We need to know where the stash house at or we'll fuck you up…shit or just kill yo' ass," he taunted with a sinister laugh.

Whether it was shock, being frozen by fear, or just willing to die, Jeff refused to say a word. The group had him handcuffed, with a hood over his head, as they continued beating him. He was punched in the face, dragged around rooms downstairs, stomped on, slammed with a chair, kicked and had his head struck against a wall. When that didn't get the desired results, they upped the torture by burning him, leaving Jeff with severe burns on several parts on his body, including his head and neck.

"This nigga done wore me out," one of the men

cracked. "I'll be back. I'ma get me something to eat."

"Hold up, I'm comin' wit' you."

"Me too."

After three of the men left, Jeff was now tied to a chair in the kitchen; his hands remained handcuffed, his feet were bound with rope and a jumper wrapped around his neck.

"Yo, maybe this is what will get this nigga right," the goon said to the other two men, producing a needle and threatened to inject Jeff with heroin.

"Nah, we need this muthafucka somewhat coherent. We give him a shot of that, he won't be able to tell us shit," the other goon joked. "I have a better idea." They pulled down Jeff's jeans to sexually humiliate him. The gang of three boiled a pot of water in front of him. Although Jeff couldn't see what was going on, he could hear the subtle commotion around him.

"We gon' give you one more chance to give up that info, or shit 'bout to get ugly." But Jeff remained silent. One of the men stuffed a sock into his mouth and taped it shut before another man poured the hot water on his torso and genitals. The pain was beyond excruciating. Jeff feared he was going to suffocate. But they quickly ripped off the tape and removed the sock, thinking finally their brutalized victim would be ready to spill the real. At this point, Jeff was gravely injured but far from dead, and kept quiet.

"Shit, now I'm wore the fuck out too. Take his ass upstairs while we get something to eat. We can continue this shit when we get back," he told one of the other men.

"A'ight, I'll be right back," he said cutting the rope from around Jeff's feet so he could walk. "You know we ain't playin' wit' you, nigga. You know what it is. You better lead us to the drugs and the money, or you won't be leaving here the same," the man spit, leading Jeff to an upstairs bedroom.

When a call came through, the man shoved Jeff into the bedroom and slammed the door shut. While the man stepped away to take the call, Jeff, still handcuffed and hooded, could feel a slight breeze coming from an open window. He decided to roll the dice and jumped out in an attempt to escape. He landed in the front of the house, with the hood covering his face ripping apart when his body hit the ground. The sight of a bloody and bruised man soon drew the attention of a passerby on a bike and two sisters walking their Pitbull. The smell of fresh human blood in the air made the Pitbull revert to his natural tendencies, they were bred to fight and if they tasted blood, it would only further their viciousness in battle.

"Help me." Those were the first words Jeff had spoken in hours.

"Canaan stop!" the sister yelled, yanking on the Pitbull's leash as he tried to pursue a blood spattered Jeff. Hearing the ruckus, a mere few feet away from the front door, prompted the men inside the house to find out what was going on. When one of the men stepped outside, it took them a moment to realize the limp body lying on the ground was their tortured hostage.

"Man, come help me get this nigga up," the goon yelled but the Pitbull wasn't about to let his prey be taken away.

"I got your text, what the fuck is going on?" Caesar questioned when he met up with Darius. "You still ain't heard from Jeff?"

"Nope. I been calling him and his phone gotta be turned off because it keeps going straight to voicemail."

"When is the last time you talked to him?"

"A few hours ago. He said he had a stop to make, which was supposed to be with one of the connects, then he was coming to me. But this nigga went ghost and he never made it to the connect," Darius revealed.

"Fuck!" Caesar shook his head, alarmed by what he was hearing. "Do you know where he was at when you spoke to him?"

"Yeah, he said he wasn't far from here…over there on Berry Road."

"Shit, let's go. I got some shooters waiting outside in the car. We can ride around in that area and find out if anybody saw anything," Caesar told Darius heading out the door.

"I have a bad feeling," Darius disclosed.

"Me too. I just pray he ain't dead because these streets done got so fuckin' grimy," Caesar sighed, mentally preparing himself for the worse.

"Hold up, go back," Darius said to the driver, noticing the custom rims on Jeff's Benz truck parked in the parking lot of the convenience store. They checked inside the store to see if he was in there but soon concluded that although Jeff's car was here, he was nowhere around. As they continued to canvass the surrounding neighborhood, they drove up on what at first appeared to be an altercation over a dog, but something didn't seem right.

"Pull over," Caesar directed. He jumped out the Escalade with his shooters trailing close behind. "Do you know what's going on over there?" he asked the teenage boy who had been riding his bike before he stopped.

"Bro, that shit was crazy. They was walking," he said pointing towards the sisters, "And I was riding my bike when we saw some guy falling out the window. I don't know if he was pushed or what. But them girl's pit wanted to attack the guy on the ground. Then some dude came out the house and they over their beefin'. I decided to stay over here, keepin' my distance 'cause that shit lookin' all bad!" the teenage boy expressed, describing the incident.

It wasn't until one of the sisters moved to the side, did Caesar get a view of the man on the ground and recognized it was Jeff. As he ran up on the chaos, the Pitbull had finished mauling a lifeless Jeff and was now attacking another man, while the sisters were screaming for Canaan to stop, but the killer dog was paying them no mind.

"Kill that muthafucka!" Caesar shouted to his shooters, who let out two shots, murdering the dog instantly. He ran over to Jeff and knelt down next to him, but his longtime friend and partner in business was clearly dead. Caesar rose up and locked eyes with the man who he essentially saved by having one of his shooters put a couple bullets in the Pitbull.

"Not Jeff!" Darius yelled out when he got to the scene and saw his friend's bloody and mangled body on the ground, with the dead dog next to him. "What tha fuck happened?!" he bawled.

"My Canaan didn't do all that," one of the sister's cried out, mourning her deceased dog. "This man was damn near dead when we walked up."

"Damn sure was," the other sister attested through tears. "He was the one that came out the house after the man fell out the window," she added, pointing to one of the goons who had kidnapped Jeff.

The goon was holding his bloody arm, maintaining his cool. He wanted to make a move, but he didn't have a weapon on him, so he had to be cautious. He was wondering why the two other men in the house hadn't come out yet to check on him, but he figured they might be waiting for backup. Caesar's men were heavily armed and could easily inflict massive damage.

"Who's responsible for this?" Caesar stepped in the goon's face and asked.

"Bro, I just got here to make a buy right before homeboy fell out the window. I don't even know that man. There was a couple niggas in the house before I arrived. They might know something," he shrugged, telling nothing but lies and Caesar knew it.

"Then why was you kickin' him...tellin' him to get the fuck up when Canaan got off his leash and ran towards you?" the sister snapped.

"Yo bitch, shut tha fuck up and mind yo' business," he barked. "You don't know what you talkin' 'bout," he scoffed, making eye contact with Caesar.

There was no need for Caesar to say a word. One of his shooters had a Glock with a switch, so he wasn't going to miss, and he aimed his gun directly at the goon's head. But he knew not to pull the trigger, because for now Caesar wanted the opp alive.

"Bro, what you doin? Don't listen to that bitch. She don't know what she talkin' 'bout," he protested.

"We'll see," Caesar bit down on his lip, itching to kill the man every time he glanced at the ground and saw Jeff's motionless body. "Go around the back and grab up whoever in that house. If anyone make a move put a bullet in they head. But try and take them alive. We gon' find out tonight who responsible for Jeff's death," he promised.

Chapter Six

Vigilante Shit

Brianna headed straight to the checkout counter when she entered the upscale boutique on Westheimer Road.

"Hi, I wanted to return this purse. It doesn't match the outfit I bought it to go with," Brianna said, handing the woman the bag and receipt.

The woman scrutinized the pricey crocodile satchel bag and then the receipt. "Not a problem, I'll refund the credit card. It should take three to five business days for the credit to appear on your card," she informed Brianna.

"You can't give me back that cash?"

"Unfortunately, not. I can only refund the payment method used to purchase the item."

"Damn, I don't want this charged back to Clayton's credit card," Brianna mumbled. When Remi heard the name Clayton, her ears perked up. She knew it could've been a total fluke, but Remi wondered if the Clayton the woman mentioned, was the same Clayton that had dealings with Crystal. She decided to try and dig a little deeper.

"Was the purse purchased with your credit card? Because if so, all I need is your name and I can perhaps give you a store credit," Remi offered.

"Ooh, now a store credit sound real cute." Brianna smiled widely. "But my boyfriend purchased the purse. His name is Clayton Collins. Is there a way for you to look his name up and still give me a store credit?"

"Honestly, that's against store policy."

"Come on, help a sista out. We're supposed to look out for each other," Brianna winked. "If you do this for me, I'll let you pick out something for yourself. Hell, they'll be more than enough coins on that store credit," she beamed, doing her best to entice the woman. But Remi didn't need enticing, unbeknownst to Brianna, she was the one fetching for information.

"You don't have to do that. Plus, that's really against store policy."

"I won't tell if you won't tell," Brianna continued smiling but noticed the woman seemed uncomfortable with her offer, so she switched it up. "If you won't let me get you something in the store, how about I take you out for dinner and drinks?"

"You are really laying it on thick," Remi giggled, amused with how persistent Brianna was.

"Girl, I need that store credit, because I don't want to keep the purse and I don't know when I'll be able to get my boyfriend back in this store. He's a very busy man."

"I understand. There's a way I can still issue the store credit and you can spend it anyway you like," Remi returned the wink.

"Girl, you are the best!! I feel like reaching over this glass and giving you a hug."

"You really are funny," Remi laughed.

"I'm dead ass serious," Brianna smacked. "How about you at least let me take you out to a fancy restaurant. Of course, my treat. You seem like a really cool chick, and I haven't been living here that long, so I need some friends," she grinned.

"Where did you move here from?"

"New York."

"Wow, that's a major difference. How are you liking it here?" Remi asked, while printing out Brianna's store credit.

"I'm loving it here actually. My ex-boyfriend got me here and my new boyfriend is what's keeping me here. So, are we doing dinner or what?"

"Dinner it is," Remi nodded, handing Brianna the card with the store credit.

"Thank you, girl!" Brianna kissed the card. "Now let me get to shopping. "I'm pretty positive, I'm about to work up an appetite, so what do you say, dinner tonight?"

"Sounds perfect," she agreed. Remi wasn't sure what would come of her dinner date with Brianna, but her gut said the woman could be a potential wealth of information that could lead to her finding Crystal. Something had to give because her best friend was missing, and she was convinced someone in the Collin's family was responsible for her disappearance. Having Clayton's girlfriend walk inside the luxury store, while she was working, didn't seem like a random coincidence but more like a golden opportunity Remi intended to take full advantage of.

"Hey!" Vannette answered out of breath. "I almost missed your call."

"You doing a lot of huffing and puffing. I know you're pregnant, but you're not that far along," Ashton joked.

"Stop it!," Vannette laughed. "I was downstairs, and I realized I left my purse up here. When I was coming back to get it, I heard my phone ringing, so I was rushing. What's going on with you?"

"I'm back home for a couple days."

The Legacy Part III

"Are you serious!!! When can I see you? I miss you so much."

"I miss you too. If you're not busy, you can come over tonight. My mom is having a small, dinner get together for me. I would love for you to come," Ashton said extending an invite.

"Of course, I want to come. Just let me know the time, and I'll be there," Vannette announced.

"Perfect. If you want, Lizzie can pick you up, since she's coming too," Ashton offered.

"That would be great. I'll give her a call when we get off the phone. She's been clutch since you've been gone. Because you know how emotional I can be when it comes to your brother."

"I know and Lizzie has actually enjoyed being your sounding board."

"Obviously nobody is a better sounding board than you, but she's a close second," Vannette laughed. "This dinner and seeing you tonight is exactly what I need. You have a way of always making me feel better."

"Yeah, we have a lot of catching up to do. So, I'll see you tonight My Love." Ashton blew Vannette a few kisses before hanging up.

After placing a call to Lizzie to confirm a pickup time, Vannette ran to her bedroom to find out what she was going to wear for the intimate dinner party tonight. She knew her baby daddy would be in attendance, so Vannette wanted to look her best. Although she was still in the early stages, that pregnancy glow was beginning to emerge, and she was hoping Clayton would notice and be drawn to her.

"Now this is giving pregnant woman sexiness." Vannette gushed over the mauve colored long sleeve, deep V-neck ruffle trim mini dress with a lace back, while staring in the full-length standing gold trim mirror.

"I don't even know what to say to his mother," Darius said, shaking his head while pacing the living room floor at Caesar's crib.

"Maybe we should fly to New York and tell her in person," Caesar suggested. "Because I don't think this is a conversation either one of us want to have over the phone.

"I agree, but one of us needs to stay here. We have that shipment from Alejo coming in tomorrow," Darius reminded him.

"Damn, I've been so fucked up over Jeff's death, I forgot about that shit. You go to New York, and I'll handle tomorrow's delivery. I hate when you go, you can't tell his mother that we took care of everyone involved in Jeff's death," Caesar sighed with a heavy heart.

"I know. Them bitch ass niggas didn't tell us shit before they got murked," Darius scoffed. "If it wasn't for the meth head's house they used, we wouldn't even know there were three other men involved with kidnapping and torturing Jeff."

"That shit pissed me off so bad but we gotta find them niggas and take them out too. But I still can't shake this feeling that them muthafuckas was just the hired help," Caesar conveyed.

"I think you're right but who?"

"Maybe a competitor," Caesar reasoned. "Remember a few months ago when Jeff said TJ told him business had been slower because we won't the only party in town no more."

"Yeah, I remember that. Because I mentioned Flint, who handles shit over in Austin, telling me there was an influx of product hittin' the streets his way too. You wanted to find out who was floodin' the streets with the extra product and eliminate them," Darius said, recalling the discussion in detail.

"Yeah, but ya shut me down," Caesar fumed. "Saying I didn't need to start a drug war and bring unwanted attention on the organization because we was making way too much money. Now look…Jeff dead."

"We don't know who responsible for what happened to Jeff. It's all speculation at this point. But we do need to focus on finding out, because if a drug war has been started, we better prepare for it asap. We don't need no more dead bodies poppin' up in Houston courtesy of our opps," Darius lamented.

Caesar knew Darius was right. Losing Jeff was enough, they did not need to add anymore dead bodies to the list. The clock was ticking, and it was do or die time. If the streets sniffed out any vulnerability within their organization, the wolves would start circling and plotting to take them out permanently.

Chapter Seven

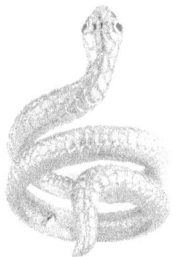

Sweet Nothing

"I didn't realize this dinner was going to be so fancy," Ashton commented admiring the Jay Strongwater orchid double candlesticks adorning the long white dining table, inlaid with gold accents that could comfortably accommodate at least ten people. The table was lighted by cluster chandeliers that hung from the luminous tray ceiling.

"Of course, it's going to be fancy. We have a lot to celebrate. My youngest child and favorite daughter is home."

"Mother, I'm your only daughter," Ashton laughed.

"I know this and besides," Karmen smiled. "We are long overdue for a reason to celebrate and put this formal dining room to use. It's a shame we rarely utilize such a beautiful space," she remarked glancing at the beige wainscoted walls, decorated with framed artworks, surrounded by open archways with mounted candle scones and a fireplace under an ornate mirror. The elegant, tufted chairs with high back features surrounded the table and through the glass sliding doors, you had a panoramic view of the massive, landscaped garden and an infinity edge pool with LED-illuminated fountains.

"I agree and I'm thrilled to be the catalyst for you using such a gorgeous formal dining room," Ashton said giving her mother a kiss on the cheek.

"I do admit, it's a bit of a letdown that your friend won't be joining us tonight. I was looking forward to meeting him."

"He's looking forward to meeting you all too. So, although he can't make it tonight, his flight will be here in the morning. Maybe the three of us can do lunch. I'm not sure if I'm ready to introduce Zephan to everyone just yet," Ashton divulged.

"I would love for the three of us to go out to lunch. I don't think I've ever met a rap superstar before," Karmen joked. "But on a more serious note, do you think your reluctance to introduce him to the family is because you haven't decided if your marriage to Damacio is actually over?"

"I think Damacio has already made that decision for both of us. He's been seeing another woman, and I don't believe he has any interest in saving our marriage," Ashton confided contritely. "I can't help but blame myself."

"I'm so sorry, Ashton. I know how much you loved Damacio. Unfortunately, it seems your kidnapping took a heavy toll on your marriage, and that's not your fault. You went through something traumatic. Sometimes that brings couples closer together, and it can also tear them apart."

"It certainly didn't help our marriage that I believe Alejo was behind my kidnapping, but Damacio chose to take the word of his father," Ashton denounced.

"I'm still incensed over the role Alejo played. But he will be dealt with. Your father has promised me that. So, I don't want you putting any energy into that man. You focus on healing mentally and physically. I can already see the positive influence the rehab facility is having on you. I'm truly proud of you," Karmen praised, holding her daughter closely.

"Thank you so much," she said, lying her head on her mother's shoulder. Ashton cherished the maternal connection she received being in her mother's arms. "Although I'm relishing in all this love you're giving me, I'm off to finish getting dressed before the guests arrive."

"Yes, I'm about to go do the same. I will see you

back here shortly," Karmen said as her daughter walked off. Karmen was headed upstairs when she noticed her husband speaking to a young, casually dressed man. Not someone she would typically see Allen socializing with, especially not at their home. She was tempted to go introduce herself, but they quickly disappeared into Allen's office.

"Why in the fuck would you show up at my home?" Allen barked, shutting his office door.

"Man, you weren't takin' my calls and when I stopped by your office, I couldn't get past security."

"If my wife wasn't having a dinner party tonight, then I wouldn't have allowed my security to leave early, and you wouldn't have made it in my home either. You should not have come here," Allen reiterated pouring himself a drink.

"Listen, I ain't have no choice. Three of my men dead behind that kidnapping and the other two wanna get out of town thinking they next. So, I need the rest of my money."

"You only had one job to do," Allen quipped. "I knew I should've hired professionals, but I figured you could handle roughing up one of Caesar's men and getting me some intel. Talk about a waste of my time and money," he exhaled shaking around the ice cubes in his glass.

"Man, that nigga Jeff was built a lil' differently than I expected. No one thought Caesar was gon' show up to the trap house wit' shooters neither. Shit just went all wrong."

Allen went to the safe he kept in his office and retrieved a few stacks, stuffing them in an envelope. "Take this, and don't come back," he told the hired goon.

"I can finish the job and take care of Caesar. All you have to do is say so."

"I'll pass. You couldn't even deliver on the first part of the job. I won't be making the same mistake twice. This time I will be hiring professional killers to take out Caesar. Now, I have a dinner party to attend, so you can see yourself out."

"Excuse me man," the goon said crossing paths with Kasir as he was leaving.

"Who was that?" Kasir asked his father when he came out his office behind the man that was leaving.

"A handyman. He was picking up some money for a job he did for me."

"I see," Kasir nodded, glancing back one more time to get a look at the man.

"I'm starving," Allen said, placing his hand on Kasir's shoulder. "Let's go eat, son."

"This is unbelievable. I thought Caesar's house was amazing, but this place is breathtakingly beautiful," Brianna gasped when Clayton drove up the circular brick and concrete driveway that was bordered with gray bricks to match the color of the elegant stone mansion. Hedge bushes and flowers planted in the center of the circle made for a beautiful entrance to the estate.

"Who is Caesar?"

"I told you about him. My ex-boyfriend."

"That's right, the one who moved you here from New York," Clayton said exiting the car.

"If it wasn't for him, I would've never met you," Brianna gushed, giving Clayton a kiss as they held hands walking into the home.

"If it's not too late, I think we better get Vannette out of here immediately," Lizzie whispered to Ashton, while they were grabbing a few hors d'oeuvres from the mirrored buffet table.

"Why, what's wrong?" Ashton asked, filling up her plate.

"Look who just walked in."

Ashton glanced up and wished she could unsee what was staring her in the face. "Is Vannette still in the restroom? Because if so, I'm going to find an excuse for us to exit out the back entrance," she said putting her plate down.

"It's too late," Lizzie sighed when Ashton was headed in the direction of the bathroom.

"This pregnancy has me peeing every damn minute," Vannette complained walking up to Lizzie and Ashton.

"I don't think I had a chance to show you the changes my mom made to the pool area. It's like an oasis. Come on let me show you," Ashton said, taking Vannette's arm leading her in the opposite direction of her brother.

"You can show me that tomorrow because girl I'm starving." Vannette freed her arm. "Right on time! They're bringing out the food now," she smiled widely. But that smile quickly faded away. She placed her hand over her stomach as if overcome with pain.

"Vannette, are you okay?" Ashton held her friend, concerned for her wellbeing.

"I need to sit down." Vannette walked over to the table to sit down in the chair with the tag holder personalized with her name. "This can't be happening to me. Why is she here?"

"Lizzie, you stay here and watch Vannette. I'll be right back." Ashton said, hurrying over to her brother, ready to throw him out.

"There she is. My baby sister is home," Clayton grinned, putting his arm out to give her a hug.

"Save it! Why would you show up with her?!" Ashton hissed.

"Her name is Brianna," Clayton retorted. "And I don't like your tone.

"Well, I don't like the fact that you're flaunting her in front of Vannette."

"First of all, I had no idea Vannette would be here. Regardless, I have the right to bring anyone I like as my dinner guest, including Brianna, who is carrying my child," Clayton shot back.

"Vannette is carrying your child too."

"Tell me something I don't already know, Ashton."

"You're such an arrogant fuck!" she snapped.

"Clayton, I'm so happy you finally got here, and I see you brought a date. You must be Brianna," Karmen said, welcoming her with a warm embrace. "It's a pleasure to meet you."

"Thank you. It's such a pleasure to meet you also. And your home is amazing. I feel so honored to be here." Brianna stated sweetly.

"I hope you enjoy the dinner and I look forward to getting to know you better," Karmen smiled. "Clayton and Ashton, I need for you all to keep your voices down. Whatever issues the two of you have, save it for later."

"I can't believe you're fine with him bringing this woman here, flaunting her..."

"Ashton, that's enough!" Karmen rarely raised her voice to her kids but when she did, they knew she meant business and it was time to shut it down. "They're bringing out our food, so let's go sit down and eat."

Ashton rolled her eyes at her brother and rushed off to check on Vannette.

"I apologize for my sister's rude behavior. She was completely out of line."

"Don't worry about it. I guess I shouldn't be surprised. She is close to Vannette," Brianna shrugged. "I'm fine though. Having your mother be so nice to me makes whatever Ashton said irrelevant."

"I like your attitude and you're absolutely right. My mother's approval is the only one that matters to me."

"Here comes trouble," Brianna commented when

she saw Vannette headed in their direction. Ashton and Lizzie both tried keeping her in the chair, but she was a woman not to be stopped.

"How could you bring her here, Clayton? I thought we had an understanding."

"Vannette, I honestly didn't know you were going to be here tonight. If I had known, I wouldn't have brought Brianna because I have no desire to bring our drama to my mother's dinner party."

"If you don't want any drama, then you should ask Brianna to leave. She has no right to be here."

"Brianna is my girlfriend, and she has every right to be here."

Clayton's words cut Vannette worse than a sharp knife. Her world had been turned upset down and there was only one person she blamed, and that was Brianna. She had played the game of seduction masterfully, leaving Vannette feeling like a defeated outsider.

"How did things go from you saying we were getting married to now Brianna being your girlfriend? That makes absolutely no sense."

"That was a mistake."

"A mistake or a convenient excuse? Because we're both pregnant with your child, you don't think you have to marry either one of us? Answer me, Clayton!" Vannette shouted.

"You need to calm down. Your behavior is erratic. If you want to know the truth, I never said I didn't want to get married, I just don't want to marry you," Clayton articulated without mercy.

"Clayton!" his father called out with authority in his voice. "It's time to come sit down. Dinner is being served."

When Clayton and Brianna went to take their seats at the table, Vannette wanted to run out the house in tears. Her heart felt stomped on. There was this immense pain that was eating up her soul. *Don't you dare fold Vannette. Fuck Brianna. She's played the game well; you just have to play better. Pull it together and stay focused. Figure out how to erase the competition. You will have the fairytale life you've always dreamed of,* Vannette promised herself.

Chapter Eight

Dangerous Love

With his Swarovski 10x42 NL pure binoculars in tow, Gustaf watched from a distance as two brothers Ramon and Jose Gamboa, high ranking members of a Mexican cartel were preparing to board a private jet with at least seven suitcases. With the clarity, brightness, field view, and chromatic aberration of the binoculars, he could clearly see the brothers were inspecting the contents of one piece of luggage which contained bricks of drugs wrapped in plastic. Shortly thereafter, a Ford pickup and two tractor trailers pulled up on the tarmac.

Alejo had ordered Gustaf to place the two brothers under twenty-four-hour surveillance for the pasts week and this was the first-time he was getting traction on the low-key smugglers. They moved in silence but when they did move it was in large volumes.

"Boss, I was just about to call you," Gustaf said, answering Alejo's call.

"Where are you?"

"The airport watching your friends. They're preparing to board a private jet as we speak. "

"Interesting, so their flight is just now getting ready to leave?"

"Initially, I thought they were leaving immediately but some other men pulled up a few minutes ago carrying their own bags. I believe it's money. What would you like for me to do?" Gustaf wanted to know.

"Let the brothers get on the plane and leave. I have a crew waiting at the airport upon their arrival. But I need you to follow the drugs. The men I sent there to assist you are in place to confiscate the product when you give them the greenlight."

"This is a massive quantity of product and money that's about to be confiscated, Alejo. Are we prepared for the repercussions that will surly follow?"

"It will not trace back to me, as they have no idea I'm aware of their dealings. Allen's son Clayton has been doing business with Jeevan, his Indian drug connect. Chaos will ensue but it will be within their own organization," Alejo reasoned. "But it will benefit our operation. Caesar mentioned to me a few months ago that he had some competition which was causing business to slow down. That's what made me start doing my own investigating because he had no idea who was moving all this product on his territory."

"If Caesar is aware of what is going on, why couldn't we have used his men for this operation?"

"Caesar is not aware, and I want to keep it that way. The least amount of people that know the better. He will soon realize business is picking back up because his unknown competitor has no product. That will be the most he knows, and he doesn't need to know anything else. Understood?"

"Yes, you're the boss. I follow your instructions," Gustaf assured him.

"Good. You let me know when the plane takes off so that I can alert the crew waiting at the arrival destination, so they can confiscate the money and of course let me know when you have the drugs," Alejo restated.

"Will do boss. I'll be in touch."

"Girl, I apologize for cancelling at the last minute, but my boyfriend wanted me to attend this dinner party with him, and you know I had to go," Brianna explained to Remi during their lunch at Artisans.

"No need, this fabulous food and drinks are enough

of an apology. But this is like my third drink, and you're still sipping on that juice. It's kinda rude to make a girl drink alone," Remi giggled.

"Trust me, I'm a drinker but in my current condition it's a no bueno for me."

"Your current condition...what's wrong with you, are you sick?"

"No, I'm pregnant!" Brianna shared her baby news with excitement.

"Congrats!! That's wonderful."

"Yes, it is, especially since the father is filthy rich," she bragged.

"You are a mess, but I love it," Remi giggled some more.

"I'm just being honest. It's much more beneficial to be carrying the child of a rich man instead of poor one. Luckily, I actually like my baby daddy too and he cute," Brianna added with a wink.

"How long have you all been together?"

"Just a few months. It was kind of a whirlwind affair, but it worked out in my favor. He does have another woman pregnant too, but she's not my problem." Brianna stated dismissively.

"It sounds like things might get complicated."

"Not for me," she shrugged. "Vannette is in her feelings because she's been dating him off and on for a long time, but they were never exclusive. She thought she'd sealed the deal by getting pregnant, but then I got pregnant too. And check this out," Brianna let out a wicked laugh. "The other night at the dinner party, he introduced me as his girlfriend and Vannette's face literally dropped. "Poor thing," she mocked.

"Well, it sounds like you have locked yourself in and you're set, at least for the next eighteen years," Remi raised up her wine glass at Brianna.

"Honestly, Remi what I learned a long time ago is that you can never really lock yourself in with a man like Clayton. They're selfish whores at heart, but if you fall back and give them space, they're more inclined to keep you around. I don't mind sharing as long as I'm getting a nice, big piece of the pie."

Remi just sat back for the next hour or so, listening to Brianna run her mouth, because the woman could talk. But she was so shamelessly honest, it was refreshing and enjoyable to hear what she had to say. Remi felt that Brianna and Crystal were a lot alike but with one major difference. Crystal was a romantic at heart. She tried to play the game but would always end up getting played herself. Brianna on the other hand, was in love with living a lavish life. Dealing with a rich man to provide it, simply made him a means to an end.

"Thank you," Karmen said graciously, handing her car key to the valet.

"You look beautiful."

Karmen turned to see if the familiar voice was who she thought it was. "Caesar, what are you doing here?"

"You really do look beautiful, but you always do," Caesar said, complimenting the mock neck silk camel colored midi dress with a side slit and a tie cinching her svelte waist.

"Thank you," Karmen blushed, although she tried not to let Caesar see by glancing in the opposite direction.

"You changed your phone number."

"I felt it was the best thing to do."

"Best for who?" Caesar asked. "It's not best for me and I know it's not best for you," he said taking Karmen's hand. His touch still sent a warm sensation throughout her body.

"Best for both of us. I'm committed to my marriage, and I don't want or need any distractions."

"Karmen, I tried to respect your decision, but Allen isn't the man you think he is. That evening I came to your home, I wanted to tell you what I learned about your husband. He…"

"Just stop right there," Karmen demanded, putting her hand up. "I don't want to hear anything you have to say about Allen."

"But you need to know. It changes everything."

"It changes nothing because I don't want to hear it," she continued to insist. "I know exactly what Allen is capable of, but he is my husband. When I decided to stay in our marriage, that meant standing by his side no matter what."

"I don't understand how you can say that. Maybe it would be easier for me to accept if we weren't in love. You're supposed to be with me Karmen, not Allen."

"Caesar, I made my choice and I need for you to respect it. No more coming to our home or showing up at places like this. If my husband sees me talking to you, there is no telling what he might do. He can be a very treacherous man," Karmen cautioned him.

"I know exactly what type of man your husband can be, but I can be equally as treacherous, especially when it comes to protecting you. I know we belong together and trust me, one day you will know it too," Caesar voiced, continuing to hold Karmen's hand.

"I have to go. Please don't contact me again." Karmen turned and walked away with her fingers slipping through Caesar's hand. He wanted to reach out and pull her back into his arms. He refused to give up as she was the only woman Caesar wanted to spend the rest of his life with. Karmen wouldn't allow him to tell her the truth, so Caesar decided he would have to show her.

Chapter Nine

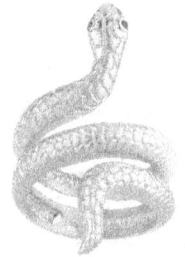

Where You Wanna Be

Clayton pulled up in his 2023 Lamborghini Urus, the Performante model with 23-inch wheels, equipped with racetrack-ready Pirelli P Zero Trofeo R rubber. This wasn't your standard exotic SUV but more of a track monster. While playing with the infotainment system and reconfigurable gauges he had the volume turned all the way up on the Bang & Olufsen sound system with Shiest Talk by Lil Baby on blast.

The Legacy Part III

Used to dream of driving foreigns, had to grab one
Of all my mamas children
I'm the bad one
I admit that
God gone have to call and tell me
To give yo shit back
I was thuggin way back before Tony put Trevor on a shit bag
Lil Juan got killed
It hit me
Been my nigga since elementary
Justin tried to make me
Go half on buddy lawyer
I wasn't wit it
All these niggas do is brag
But go out bad
I just don't get it
They be poppin on the gram
But they can't pop out in my city
Every charge I had dismissed
Swallow my kid
You don't get no kiss
Ion play games
But a nigga send blitz
Everything change when a nigga get rich
Glock with a switch
How a nigga gone miss...

Clayton was far from a street nigga but in many

ways, he encompassed the same survival traits they utilized. So, anytime business became tumultuous he would keep certain music on repeat because it motivated him to stay focused and go harder. And for his meeting with Jeevan, it was imperative he zeroed in on what the fuck was really going on.

By the way Jeevan, was sitting at the table surrounded by his typical bevvy of beauties, sipping champagne, you would think it was business as usual. However, Clayton was in no mood for pussy or drinks. He wanted to discuss business not bitches.

"Here's my favorite guy. Ladies say hello to my dear friend Clayton," Jeevan cheered. The women gladly did as they were told. "Have a seat my friend. Let me pour you a drink."

"I'm good," Clayton declined. "Tell me what is going on, Jeevan. My men have no product and I have no money."

"Yes, yes. Are you sure you don't want to eat first before we discuss business?"

"I'm positive."

"Ladies, please excuse us. We have business to discuss," Jeevan told the women who scurried off with their bottles of champagne without hesitation. "Clayton, there was some sort of mishap. I'm not sure what happened. The men made the normal exchange for the product, but their trailer was stopped, and someone took all the drugs. And the same thing happened with the money. Soon after their flight landed in California, they too were robbed. Very strange," Jeevan shook his head, taking a bite of the cocktail shrimp.

"You have no idea who robbed you?"

"No. It's all very strange."

"Was it an inside job with your people...have you investigated?" Clayton wanted to know.

"I've been dealing with these people for many years, never had any issue. Sometimes these sorts of things happen, Clayton. It's part of our business. Hopefully, we won't have this problem ever again." Jeevan stated nonchalantly.

"So, are you going to reimburse me my money or reup on the drugs? I prefer the product, but I'll take the money," Clayton exhaled deeply.

"Clayton, this comes with the territory. We call it the hazardous fund. You can't possibly expect for me to refund you when my people were robbed. This was not my fault. I lost money too."

"I gave you the money for your product, now I have neither. You need to make that right, Jeevan."

"I tell you what, I'll give you a deep discount. We've done great business together. I don't want you to feel slighted."

Clayton was furious. He wanted to punch that annoying smirk off Jeevan's face. He was in the position to take these types of loses, but Clayton had gone all in with his own money for this buy, in an attempt to finally break away from his father. But this robbery set him back and now he would have to wait to set up shop on his own.

"How long will it take you to replace my product?" Clayton asked, ready to set up Jeevan to be robbed his damn self but he had to think logically. His drugs were excellent, the prices were decent and up until now, Jeevan had always been reliable with delivery. Without a replacement, Clayton knew he needed to keep their business relationship intact.

"Elesia, get the door!" Damacio yelled out from the bathroom. While in the shower, he could see from the high-tech security system installed that a courier was there trying to make a deliver.

"Sure." Elesia was pretty much always naked while lounging around the house, so she threw on one of Damacio's t-shirts and went downstairs. "Can I help you?"

"Yes, I have a delivery for Damacio Hernandez. Can you sign for it?"

"Yes, I'm his girlfriend." Her condescending tone did not go unnoticed while signing for the package. Elesia closed the door and took it upon herself to open the envelop to see what was inside. Her eyes began to dance, feeling like she was receiving an early Christmas present.

Damacio was out the shower and sitting on the bed when Elesia came back in the bedroom skimming through some papers. "Is there a reason you opened my package?" he asked taking the documents out of Elesia's hand.

"I didn't think you would mind. I am your girlfriend."

Damacio briefly wondered how within a few short months Elesia went from a casual companion to a full-fledged live-in girlfriend. He couldn't spend much time contemplating that due to being unsettled by what he was reading.

"What is this bullshit." Damacio griped.

"It appears the Mrs. is ready to cut ties and move on. Isn't that why people typically serve divorce papers on their spouse," she shrugged.

Damacio promptly called Ashton, but it went to voicemail. "She needs to answer her fuckin' phone!" he barked; furious his wife served him divorce papers without advance warning.

"I'm not sure why you're so surprised by this. She was frolicking around on a beach with another man, and you are living with another woman."

"Elesia would you do me a favor and shut the fuck up. You're not telling me anything that I don't already know."

"Fine, but you need to relax. It's probably for the best your wife is putting an end to a marriage that appears to be in name only. Unless I'm missing something."

Damacio wouldn't admit it to Elesia but he knew she had valid points. Him and Ashton were living two separate lives. It became a matter of when one of them would file for divorce, not if. Yet, Damacio hadn't mentally prepared himself for such a permanent solution. But Ashton had now left him no choice.

Chapter Ten

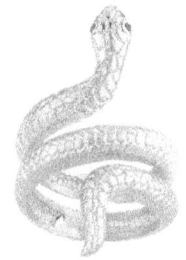

Anyone Who Had A Heart

Vannette woke up with excruciating back pain. To the point, she had to grapple with getting out the bed. She was overcome with dizziness, wooziness and feeling faint. When she made it to the restroom there was a brown discharge in her panties. It resembled coffee grounds. The discharge was actually blood that had been in her uterus for a while and was just coming out slowly.

"This can't be happening," Vannette sobbed, searching on her phone for signs of a miscarriage. In her heart, she was perfectly aware what was happening to her body but her desire to be pregnant with Clayton's baby superseded her common sense. Vannette spent the next few hours lying on the bathroom floor waiting for the pain to go away while grieving losing her baby with the man she dreamed of spending the rest of her life with.

Brianna was searching for a pen in the area where Clayton had created a makeshift office area, when she came across a piece paper. The top of the paper had the name Crystal with dates, and what appeared to be various payment amounts. Brianna continued to scrutinize the information that was scribbled in Clayton's handwriting.

"What has you over there preoccupied?" Clayton sought to find out when he saw how distant Brianna appeared.

"Who is Crystal and why did you make all these payments to her?" Crystal was holding up the paper, demanding clarification.

"Oh, that's nothing." Clayton reached over to take the paper from Brianna's hand, but she was not letting go.

"Nothing is not gonna cut it. Who the fuck is Crystal?" Brianna felt more emboldened to ask questions and make demands of Clayton now that she was carrying his child. She planned to use her new status as the current favorite future baby mama to her advantage.

"It's nothing for you to worry about, now give me that paper."

"Clayton, I'm not giving you shit. I want to know who Crystal is and why you hittin' her off with money. Are you about to have a baby with this bitch too?!" Brianna wasn't letting up with the interrogation.

"Hell no! It's nothing like that."

"Then what's it like? I need to know Clayton or I'm leaving," she threatened.

Clayton did not want to discuss his Crystal dealings with Brianna, but he also didn't want her walking out on him. He had developed a soft spot for her. It might've had something to do with them now having sex on a regular basis without using a condom, since he had no concerns of getting her pregnant. He was able to get the full experience of her wet pussy on his dick and the shit felt spectacular.

"Baby, you can relax. Crystal is someone I had done some business with."

"What sort of business?" Brianna pressed, feeling she had the upper hand. "Fine, let me get my shit, so I can go!" she smacked.

Clayton gave in under the pressure. "She was a young lady I hired to seduce my father," he hated to admit.

"You hired a woman to seduce your father...what sort of Young and the Restless, soap opera bullshit is this?!"

"I know it's crazy but at the time I felt it needed to be done. Promise me you won't repeat what I just told you to anyone."

"I promise. You can count on me to go to the grave with your secret," Brianna pledged.

"Thanks baby." Clayton kissed his woman feeling aroused and ready to slide inside until he saw Vannette calling. He ignored her the first few times, but she kept calling back. "Hold on for a minute. Hello."

"Clayton, can you please come be with me?"

"What happened? You sound like you've been crying."

"I just left the doctor's office. I had a miscarriage," she announced with tears streaming down her face.

"What! When did this happen?"

"Yesterday when I woke up, I was in a lot of pain and there was some spotting. I slept for most of the day but this morning the pain hadn't gone away, so I came in to see my doctor. She examined me and confirmed what I pretty much knew."

"Damn, I'm sorry to hear that Vannette. Did the doctor say you were okay?"

"Yes, she said I would be fine. She gave me a prescription for some pain pills and told me to go home and get some rest. Will you come see me? I really don't feel like being alone."

"I don't think I'll be able to make it today. I'll try to stop by tomorrow."

"But I lost our baby. Don't you want to be here with me?"

"Things happen, Vannette. It wasn't meant to be. The doctor told you to get some rest. I'll call and check on you tomorrow," Clayton said and ended the call.

"Vannette lost the baby?" Brianna wanted to confirm.

"Yep. It probably came from all that screaming and yelling she was doing. I told her to calm her ass down, now look what happened. But at least we still have our baby," Clayton grinned pulling Brianna close kissing her. That kiss led to another kiss, which led to a full-blown passionate tongue exchange, that had them in bed naked having sex and forgetting all about Vannette and her miscarriage.

"Did you tell your parents I said thank you, because you're all mine and they did a very good job creating you," Zephan said licking Ashton's nipples, while they laid in bed listening to his latest music release.

"I didn't repeat those exact words, but I assured them we were making each other extremely happy."

"That's a start. Now all I need you to do is get a divorce, so everyone doesn't think I'm runnin' around fuckin' a married woman."

"You are a fuckin' mess!" Ashton laughed. "But we are on the right path. Damacio got served divorce papers a couple weeks ago. Now all I have to do is wait for him to sign them."

"How long do it take a muthafucka to sign some papers?"

"Not long but he didn't sign for them when they were delivered, some woman did, so he might be out of town. I'm sure he'll sign them soon and get it back to me. I think Damacio is just as anxious as I am to officially bring an end to this marriage."

"That nigga lost is my gain because when we get married, I ain't neva letting you go. We together for life," Zephan made clear.

"I feel the same way. We together for life, babe." Ashton could not decipher if she was in lust, love or infatuated with Zephan, but she didn't care either way. Feeling wanted by him and not fixating on why her marriage failed with Damacio was what mattered most to her right now. Battling her inner demons left Ashton's self-esteem shattered, her love affair with Zephan was building it back up.

Chapter Eleven

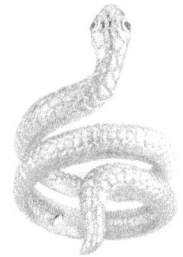

Confessions

"I understand you told me this might take some time, but you still don't have any updates?" Kasir questioned Kenneth Price, the private investigator he hired to locate Crystal.

"Not yet. She was last seen near a parking garage where she lived. I've been trying to go through any surveillance camera footage I can get ahold of, based on the last time there was cell phone activity. Again, these things take time, but I promise you I will find your friend."

"Crystal is more than a friend. She is very important to me, and I need to know what happened to her," he stressed.

"I understand, Kasir."

"We'll, talk later," he said rushing Kenneth off the phone when he saw his brother coming into his office. "Clayton, good afternoon."

"What's going on? I hope I'm not the reason you hurried off the phone," Clayton commented, sitting down on the couch.

"If it's not about making money, I'm sure you don't care what I have going on."

"Typically, that might be true, but I've been concerned about you. Lately, you've been a bit off. I know something is going on with you...talk to me."

Kasir appreciated his brother showing concern and welcomed using him as a sound board. "You know I'm worried about Crystal, and I want to find her."

"Certainly. You've never denied being completely enamored with that woman."

"It's more than that. I'm convinced something happened to her and I need answers."

"Does that mean you weren't being authentic when you said you believed our father had nothing to do with Crystal's disappearance?"

"I'm not sure what to believe." Kasir raised up from his chair, visibly frustrated. "If I have to be completely transparent with you, I don't trust our father anymore. He is beyond unscrupulous."

"Are you making moves to find out either way what is going on?"

"I am. I hired a very savvy private investigator."

"Sounds like you're taking a page out of our father's playbook," Clayton noted.

"I am." Kasir acknowledged. "I never denied our father is highly intelligent and resourceful."

"Has this private investigator come up with anything useful?" Clayton wanted to know for his own self-serving reasons. No one could ever find out that he was the one that brought Crystal into their father's life in the first place. That was a secret he wanted bury with him. Clayton felt forced to share the information with Brianna, but it needed to end with her.

"Unfortunately, not and it's infuriating. I know the truth is out there and I won't stop until I find it."

"Whatever I can do to help, I will. I know you care a great deal about her, and you deserve answers."

"Thank you, Clayton. Your support is valued. Enough about me and my nonexistent love life. How are things with you? Has the nervousness kicked in with you having two babies by two different women on the way?"

"You must haven't spoken with our mother, Vannette had a miscarriage."

"Oh wow, I'm sorry, Clayton. I'm sure Vannette is shattered."

"She's hurt but it wasn't meant to be."

"That's one way of looking at it but I doubt Vannette

sees it that way."

"You're probably right. But I have another child on the way, and I need to focus on that. You're the first to know, but I'm going to propose to Brianna. I already bought the ring."

"Congrats lil' bro!" Kasir hugged his brother. "I really am happy for you. I never thought you would get married."

"I wasn't in a rush, but I first considered it when Vannette initially told me she was pregnant. I wasn't going to marry her for love, it was me trying to do the right thing for our child. That didn't happen though because I found out Brianna was pregnant too. My feelings for Brianna are different though. I want to marry her because I do love her and I want us to raise a family together," Clayton confessed.

"My little brother has really matured and it's beautiful to see. I'm proud of you."

Kasir was proud of his brother. He was getting married and starting a family with a woman he loved. He knew that sort of stability would prove beneficial in Clayton's personal and professional life. He yearned to have that too. The problem was, Kasir wanted to share that life with a woman out of his reach.

"Hey you! We wanted to come over and bring you some

treats and see how you were doing." Ashton and Lizzie had comfort food, flowers and a stuff animal in hand.

"Thank you, ladies." Vannette was grateful for the company. She had spent the last couple weeks moping around becoming depressed. Having her friends stop by lifted her spirits.

"I know it's going to take time but are you starting to feel better?" Lizzie asked taking a bite of one of the cupcakes they brought over.

"A little. The good news is my doctor said the miscarriage didn't cause any permanent damage and I should have no problems getting pregnant again."

"That is wonderful!" Ashton and Lizzie both expressed delight with the promising news.

"Yeah, I can't wait to tell Clayton we can try again to have a baby together." Vannette caught Ashton and Lizzie exchanging disillusioned glimpses at one another. "Is there anything you all want to tell me?"

"I was planning on waiting because you're dealing with a lot but," Ashton was holding back, dreading to be the one to give Vannette the news.

"Will you please tell me what's going on?"

"Clayton and Brianna are engaged. They're getting married. I'm sorry you have to hear this, especially so soon after your loss."

Vannette grabbed the fuzzy blanket she kept on the couch and wrapped it around her arms and chest. It was a way to soothe her anxiety. "Of course, he's marrying Brianna, he wants to do right by his child. Now that I'm no longer pregnant, he doesn't have to take our baby into consideration."

"Of course, that's what it is," Ashton agreed not wanting to bring anymore heartache to her friend.

"He doesn't love her," Vannette mumbled, telling herself whatever she needed to hear to cope with losing her baby and the man she loved. But Vannette's denials could only protect her from facing reality for so long. At some point, she would have to admit the truth, Clayton never loved her, and he never would.

"Remi, it's so great to see you!"

"It's great to see you too! That pregnancy glow is in full effect and you're starting to show," she beamed patting Brianna's budding belly. "You really look gorgeous pregnant."

"Thank you and I actually feel sexier. I know that may sound crazy."

"No, it doesn't. I mean you really do look amazing."

"I think me feeling sexier is because Clayton can't keep his hands off me," Brianna laughed. "We've gotten closer than ever.

"I see! Look at the freakin' rock on your finger!" Remi held up Brianna's hand to get a closer look at the brilliant cut diamond adorning her finger. It was what would be described as an internally flawless diamond.

"Yes, Clayton proposed, and I accepted, we're getting married."

"I'm so happy for you. It's all happening so fast. Are you feeling overwhelmed, even a little?"

"Not at all. It's crazy because a few weeks ago I thought Clayton had another woman knocked up and I was ready to walk out the door, and now we're engaged."

"Why did you think he had another woman pregnant?" Remi inquired.

"Because I found this paper with this woman's name Crystal on it. There were numerous dates where he gave her these large sums of money. I thought maybe she was pregnant, and he was making payments."

"When you confronted him what did he say?"

"The payments had nothing to do with a romantic relationship. She had done some work for him." Brianna was about to go into further details but remembered the promise she made to her future husband and kept her mouth shut.

"What sort of work for such large payments?"

"Something to do with his father's corporation," Brianna lied and said. "The good news is, I was wrong about the woman Crystal. I'm the only one carrying Clayton's child and we're getting married. My life is picture perfect. Now where are those shoes I ordered. I can't wait to put them on!" she exclaimed.

Initially, Remi's incentive to befriend Brianna was because of her ties to Clayton. She wanted to see if she could find out what if any connection Clayton had with

Crystal and her disappearance. But soon those intentions changed, she found herself genuinely liking Brianna, although that didn't stop her from wanting to find out the truth about Crystal. So, when Brianna mentioned her friend, Remi finally felt she was about to get that missing piece of the puzzle. But the information she received; it wasn't earth shattering.

Maybe Clayton was making payments to Crystal on his father's behalf, or maybe he really did hire her for some sort of job. Whatever it was, Remi decided she was no longer going to use her relationship with Brianna to dig up information on Clayton. She could see how truly excited Brianna was about her life and sharing it with the father of her child and the man she loved. Remi wanted to celebrate Brianna's good fortune not try to tarnish it.

Chapter Twelve

Death Around The Corner

"Mr. Collins, you have a call from Kenneth Price," Kasir's assistant informed him.

"Put it through. Kenneth hi. Why didn't you call me on my cell phone?"

"I did but it went straight to voicemail. I realize you said that is your preferred method of me getting in touch with you, but this was too important to wait. I have some information for you," the private investigator Kasir hired told him.

"Did you find Crystal?" Kasir was gripping the phone, praying the answer would be yes.

"I did locate Crystal."

"Thank God. Where is she…do you have a contact number?"

"She's at the Houston Methodist Hospital. She's been there for weeks."

"What…and they didn't contact anybody?"

"When the paramedics brought Crystal in, she was unconscious, and she had no identification on her. Because they were unable to identify her, a notification could not be made. She's been there as a Jane Doe."

"Unconscious…what happened and has she regained consciousness yet?"

"All I know is she was shot, and her condition isn't good. I suggest you get to the hospital as soon as possible."

"Thank you, I'm on my way now." Kasir hung up with the private investigator and immediately left his office, calling Remi as he headed to the hospital.

"What tha fuck does this nigga want," Caesar huffed when he saw Pedro's number come up. "Man, didn't I tell you not to call me until you had Chi."

"I have Chi and something even better," Pedro said.

"I don't mean his whereabouts because you been saying that shit for months now. I'm talkin' about physically having him in your custody."

"That's why I'm calling you," Pedro said in a low tone.

"Yo, I need you to speak up!" Caesar shouted. "Your voice going in and out."

"I don't want anyone to hear me," Pedro said opening the screen door to go outside. "I'm at this house on Homewood Lane and not only is Chi here, but his partner, the one who tried to rape that young woman. If you want them, this is your opportunity to get them."

"Hell yeah I want them. I don't care what you have to do, don't let them muthafuckas leave. I'ma gather my men and we on the way. Drop me your location."

"I got you," Pedro said wanting to get back in Caesar's good graces.

"Are they strapped and how many men are with them?" Caesar wanted to make sure his shooters were prepared and not ambushed.

"It's just Chi and the other man, Delancey," Pedro informed him. "I don't see any weapons, but I would come with the assumption that they are carrying."

"You right. We headed that way now. Keep 'em there but text me if anything changes."

Caesar and his men rushed to the house on Homewood Lane. It was located in the heart of the Houston Hispanic Cultural Center. Pedro had advised them to walk up and come through the one car garage because Chi and Delancey were in the backyard smoking.

"Delancey is the one sitting at the table," Pedro let Caesar know before they headed to the back. "Chi is standing by the grill."

"Good looking out." Caesar had two men in front of him and another two behind him. They were each carrying an AR-15 but he was carrying something else. When they were about to enter the backyard, Chi was standing by the grill and first noticed the gang of Black men storming through the door. When Delancey turned to see what had his partner's attention, he was met with an Axe Bat Avenge Pro carbon composite baseball bat smashing the left side of his face. Caesar put all his muscle behind the swing that fractured the man's jaw.

"Que mierda esta pasado? No me mates, por favor," Chi pleaded.

"That's for Ashton, you fuckin' bum!" Caesar fumed. "Throw both of them in the back of the truck," he ordered his men. Delancey appeared to be in shock seeing his blood and teeth spilling out his mouth, but Caesar had so much more in store for the man who attempted to rape Karmen's daughter.

When Kasir reached Crystal's hospital room, his heart dropped. He initially thought she was dead because her body was completely still. But as he got closer, he could see she was breathing but barely. He went over to her bed and knelt down beside her, taking her hand.

"Crystal, it's me Kasir." He spoke in a comforting tone, wanting to reach the woman he had so much love for. It took a few moments but after several minutes her heavy eyes began to open.

"Kasir, you found me." Crystal's voice was weak, and her mouth extremely dry. Simply speaking a few words took more strength than she had to give.

"You don't have to talk. Just being here next to you is enough for me," Kasir assured her.

"No. I don't have much longer. I can feel my body shutting down," Crystal whispered

Kasir couldn't stop the tears from swelling in his eyes as he realized the woman he loved and had been searching for was dying right in front of him.

"Baby, please save your strength."

"No, before I die, I need you to know something. I really did fall in love with you. I'm sorry I left, but my past had caught up to me."

"It's okay," Kasir smiled, stroking her hand.

"No, it's not okay. I wish I would've told you the truth instead of running away, but I didn't want you to hate me."

"I could never hate you, Crystal."

"You father was the married man I was seeing, but

I was never in love with him. I only love you."

"And I love you too."

"Then get justice for me because he's the reason why I'm about to die," she revealed.

"Wait...what? You're saying my father is the one who shot you?"

"It was Jackson. He had Jackson shoot me," Crystal said making the revelation, literally on her deathbed. "He left me for dead. Your father thought I would cause him trouble. He wanted to make sure you never found out the truth about us."

"Baby, I'm so sorry," Kasir choked back tears, kissing Crystal on her forehead. "I will make sure my father pays for what he did to you."

"You promise?"

"I promise," Kasir vowed. As he knelt back down to stare Crystal directly in her eyes, that dreadful sound of when there is an absence of any detectable electrical activity of the heart muscle was heard. There was a straight line on the monitor, with absolutely no heartbeat. It had flatlined and Crystal was dead. Just then, Remi came rushing through the door.

"Finally! They sent me to the wrong hospital room," Remi said sounding out of breath as if she had been running. "How's my girl?"

Before Kasir could respond, the doctor and nurses swarmed the room, telling them to get out. They began cardiopulmonary resuscitation and injection of vasopressin, but it was all in vain. Crystal was dead and there was no bringing her back to life.

"Can someone please tell me what's going on?" Remi cried out, but in her head, she knew the answer, her heart wasn't ready to accept it. "Kasir, say something...please tell me I'm not too late."

"She's gone. Crystal is gone." Remi buried her head in Kasir's chest and they both broke down in tears. They had been on this journey together to find Crystal and now they had reached the end of the road and she had become their fallen angel. While they held each other to ease their pain, Kasir remembered the promise he made to the woman he loved before she died, and he planned to keep his word. His father would pay the price for Crystal's demise.

Chapter Thirteen

Deadly Obsession

Brianna drove up to 3488 Avalon Place thrilled to do an empty house walkthrough of the new home she would be sharing with her future husband. She had to pinch herself, because she couldn't believe that in less than a year, she was living a life beyond her wildest dreams. Not only was she pregnant with Clayton's baby, but they were also now engaged, and he purchased the most beautiful River Oaks masterpiece, where they would raise their family.

The French modern design with clean lines, lots

of windows and light, was perfect for today's modern style of living. Custom flooring with unique skylight feature in the entryway. Nine-inch white oak flooring, climate-controlled wine room, Lutron lighting system, 3-story elevator. Brianna wasn't much of a cook, but she was tempted to take classes and learn due to the opulent kitchen. The quartz countertops, expansive island, Miele suite of appliances including a built-in espresso system. The Primary bedroom on the 2nd floor had a Mediterranean meet contemporary fireplace in the sitting area, spa-like bathroom with mosaic tile flooring, Calcutta vanity counters, and a showcase closet that resembled boutique-style planning. There were three more exquisitely designed ensuites for them to fill with more babies. The 3rd floor was fully equipped with an elaborate theater, a wet bar and adjoining flex room. The final touch was a sparkling pool and outdoor kitchen, so they could do plenty of entertaining. She loved that Clayton didn't cut any corners when purchasing them their dream home.

Brianna held onto the curved glass and wood handrail, with engineered powder coated steel stringers. She felt as if she was spiralin' up, like a rich niggas staircase. But nothing prepared the bourgeoning beauty for what was waiting for her at the top of the stairs.

"Surly, you didn't think I was going to let a calculating bitch like you steal my life."

"Vannette, what the hell are you doing here and how did you get in my house?!"

"This is not your house, you fuckin' jezebel. And you will never enjoy living here. Not even for a single day," Vannette wailed, reaching into her cream tote bag to retrieve her CZ P-09 that was equipped with a suppressor and Picatinny rail. This deadly piece of artillery had unrivaled factory mags that gave 21-round capacity and Vannette wanted to unload them all on Brianna, her sworn enemy.

"Vannette, wait." Brianna swallowed hard, shaken to the core at the sight of a gun being brandished in her face. She wanted to back down the stairs but between her fear and the height of her heels, she was afraid she would trip and fall. "Please don't do this," Brianna begged, hoping she could persuade an unhinged Vannette to put the gun away.

"Now you want to beg for mercy. It's too late to humble yourself, Brianna."

"What about Clayton, you love him. You wouldn't kill his unborn baby."

"Don't worry about Clayton. I'll be there to comfort him. With you out the picture, we can finally be together, and start our own family. The family you tried to destroy."

Brianna convinced herself she could reach her former friend. She spoke, her voice a soft plea, "Vannette, don't do this to me...please."

Vannette ignored her pleading. She leveled the gun at Brianna's chest. The cold metal was growing increasingly heavy as her grip tightened. Now die!"

Vannette screamed, unloading a succession of bullets. A stunned glare was still etched on Brianna's face as her bloody body fell backwards down the spiral staircase.

"You stupid bitch! I warned you not to fuck with me," Vannette scoffed, when she reached the bottom of the stairs. She yanked off the diamond engagement ring Clayton had placed on Brianna's finger only a few short weeks ago. She decided to also take her other jewelry and wallet to give the impression this was a robbery gone wrong, that ended in murder. Once she was done, Vannette stepped over the pool of blood surrounding Brianna's dead body and snuck out the back door, leaving no trace she was ever there.

Vannette went from committing cold blooded murder to meeting Ashton and Lizzie for lunch. "Hello ladies!" she beamed, giving both women a hug.

"Hey!" Ashton and Lizzie said in unison.

"I'm so happy you came out. I was worried you were going to cancel like you did the last time," Ashton said handing Vannette a menu.

"Of course, we would've understood if you did," Lizzie added. "You've had to deal with a lot lately. How are you feeling?"

"I'm actually feeling wonderful."

"Really?" Ashton and Lizzie both stared at each other. "I'm thrilled to hear that but a bit surprised based on how you sounded just a few days ago," Ashton said raising an eyebrow.

"I know. I mean don't get me wrong, I'm still completely devastated by the loss of my baby. It's been almost three months now and the heartache continues to linger. Then for Clayton to become engaged to Brianna so soon after the loss of our child was almost unbearable," Vannette sighed, putting her head down.

"My brother can be so cruel." Ashton placed her hand on Vannette's arm, gently stroking it. "You didn't deserve any of that. I know Brianna will soon be a member of our family and according to my mother she already is," she rolled her eyes. "But that woman gives me vulture vibes. Totally out for self."

"I agree," Lizzie nodded. "But eventually she'll get hers. Those types always get a visit from karma."

"I hope you're right, Lizzie," Vannette smiled sweetly, knowing Brianna had already paid the ultimate price. "Enough about Clayton and Brianna, how are things going with you and Zephan? Are you about to be the wife of a rap superstar!" her eyes were wide with excitement.

"Maybe so. He wants to get married as soon as my divorced is finalized."

"Speaking of getting your divorce finalized, how is that going…have you heard anything from Damacio? Did he finally sign the papers?" Lizzie questioned.

"We did speak briefly on the phone the other day. I'm supposed to stop by and see him tomorrow, so we can discuss the pending divorce," Ashton informed her friends.

"I have to admit, I might be in the minority, but I really loved you and Damacio together," Vannette professed. "You all just had this chemistry, so dynamic together. I'm a little bummed it didn't work out. But Zephan is no slacker. You're going from hot to hot," she laughed.

"Well, I totally think Zephan is a better fit for you. He allows you to be yourself. Damacio was so judgmental. He came across more like your father than a husband," Lizzie frowned. "You're still young. Now you can travel around the world touring with Zephan and just have some fun!"

"Yeah, about that tour, make sure you put a couple tickets to the side for us," Vannette nodded, high-fiving Lizzie.

"You all are so funny, but you know I got you. I need my girls on the road with me," Ashton giggled. "Oh, hold on, this is my mom. Hey mom!"

"Ashton, you need to get home," her mother said in a somber tone.

"What's wrong...why do you sound so grim?"

"It's your brother."

"Did something happen to Kasir or Clayton...what happened?"

"Brianna is dead." Ashton could hear her mother's voice crack and that she was crying.

"No! What happened?"

"I don't have all the details but supposedly there was a break in at their new house and Brianna was shot and killed. Your brother is completely devastated. He needs his family. Please come home."

"I'm on my way!"

"Ashton, what happened? Whatever it is, it sounded serious," Lizzie said, putting her drink down.

"It is. I can't believe I'm about to say this. Brianna is dead."

"No fuckin' way!" Lizzie's mouth had dropped and remained wide open.

"That's horrible," Vannette shook her head. "I had my issues with her, but never would I want her to die. Do they know what happened?"

"I don't have all the details, but I have to get home to my family. Omigod, and the baby. Clayton has loss Brianna and his unborn child." That part of the devastating news finally hitting Ashton. "I have to go. I'll call you guys later."

Lizzie watched with despair as Ashton rushed out the restaurant. She now felt somewhat guilty for making a prediction of karma paying Brianna a visit. Never did she believe it would be of this magnitude and so soon. The sudden and shocking news left Lizzie in a daze. While she was sincerely dismayed, Vannette pretended to be upset. She even mustered up a few tears to make it seem real. But on the inside, her heart was filled with joy knowing Brianna was forever out of their lives.

Chapter Fourteen

Time Kills

"Clayton, I'm so sorry." Ashton ran over to her brother and held him tightly. "We'll get through this...as a family."

"Thank you. I truly appreciate you coming and being here for me."

"There's no other place I would want to be. You're my brother. I will always be here for you."

Karmen and Kasir observed from a distance as Ashton did her best to comfort her brother.

"I'm glad your sister came. Clayton needs all of our support. I'm not sure if he'll ever get over this."

"For sure. This is a tough one. I don't understand how something like this even happens. Does the police have any leads?" Kasir questioned his mother.

"No, they think it was a robbery. Brianna's engagement ring, jewelry and wallet were all stolen. Unfortunately, because they had yet to move in, the security cameras weren't set up, so the police don't have much to go off of."

"Baby, I have to step out for a couple hours. Are you going to be okay?" Allen asked his wife as Kasir stared at his father in disgust. Exercising self-control was proving to be difficult for their eldest child, but he knew under the current circumstances it was best to refrain from confronting his father about the role he played in Crystal's death. He wasn't sure how much longer he could keep the information under wraps. But Kasir also wanted to figure out how he would make his father pay.

"Kasir, don't forget we're having our annual board meeting next Friday. I wanted you and Clayton to go over the final numbers before the board met, but you might have to handle it on your own. I don't think your brother will be up to it," Allen said, noticing how distraught he appeared to be while sitting with Ashton.

"I'll take care of it," Kasir assured him. "Although knowing Clayton, he might want to throw himself into work to keep his mind off of losing Brianna and the baby."

"Honestly, I wish you were right," Allen noted. "But

I don't see him bouncing back from this anytime soon."

"I agree with your father," Karmen remarked to Kasir. To lose Brianna in such a tragic way, it will be challenging for him to recover from that. Then, he went from expecting two babies to now having none."

"Maybe you should urge Clayton to stay here with us for a while," Allen suggested. "Being around his family will be more beneficial than being at home alone. Just consider it," he told his wife, giving her a kiss before heading out.

"How have things been going between you and dad?" Kasir inquired once his father left.

"We're in a good place. I know you tend to worry about me but besides my sadness over Brianna and their unborn child, I'm doing very well, so don't be concerned. If anything, I'm concerned about you."

"Why?"

"You've been standoffish for weeks. I know it's because of the Crystal situation, but I wish you would let it go. Your father said he had nothing to do with her disappearance and I believe him, and so should you."

"Even with all the lies he has told you; you still defend him. That amazes me."

"Your father has his flaws but he's a good man and he truly loves us. Everything he does, is to protect his family. I hope you believe that. Don't allow this woman to tear our family apart. Because in the big scheme of things, we only have each other," Karmen reminded her son. "I'll be back. I'm going to check on your brother.

Kasir was left feeling torn after his mother's departing words. Loyalty and keeping the family close had been instilled in him since he was a little boy. But he felt betrayed by his father and wanted to keep his promise to a dying Crystal. If he did honor his promise to Crystal, he was aware that it could potentially alienate him from his entire family. Was getting justice for Crystal worth that. That was a question Kasir would need to answer very soon.

"I don't understand why you just don't sign those divorce papers. They've been sitting on this table for the last two weeks collecting dust," Elesia complained. "What's the hold up?"

"There is no hold up," Damacio denied.

"Great! Then you can go ahead and sign them right now," she pressed, getting a pen from the kitchen drawer and handing it to Damacio. "Sign them."

"What are you doing...why are you acting like that?"

"Like what? A woman who no longer wants to date a married man."

"We both know my marriage is over and at this point it's just paperwork. Legal matters can take time," Damacio explained.

"Not an uncontested divorce. It's as simple as you

placing your signature on the dotted line," she pointed out.

"Ashton is stopping by the club tomorrow for us to talk. I'll sign the papers then." He brushed past Elesia walking out the kitchen and she followed close behind him to the upstairs bedroom.

"What do you all need to talk about? She's moved on with Zephan and you've moved on with me. Or is it that you haven't actually moved on and you're hoping the two of you will get back together? Answer me!" she pressed Damacio for a response.

"Where is all this coming from? My marriage with Ashton is over and I'm not interested in getting back with her."

"It's good to know. I was starting to think maybe you were delaying signing the divorce papers to prevent her from marrying Zephan," Elesia reckoned, slipping off the white t-shirt she was wearing of Damacio's and crawling back into bed.

"Why would you think they're planning on getting married?" Damacio probed, while being mindful to maintain an even-tempered mood.

"They were on Instagram Live together. Zephan made the comment that once his baby's divorce was finalized, she would be taking his last name. He even showed the engagement ring he bought her," Elesia was delighted to share the news. "So, when will I be getting my ring?" the lingerie model inquired. "Maybe it's time for us to start planning our wedding," she inferred, while sprinkling kisses down his neck, shoulder and back.

"I didn't realize you were interested in getting married. You never mentioned it before."

"I can't prance around in my panties forever. I think I'm ready to get married and have a baby immediately. Don't you want a little Damacio running around?"

"Yes, I do," Damacio acknowledged. Elesia's question made him reflect on a conversation he had with Ashton before they got married.

"Ashton, how long do you plan on poppin' pills and drinking? Eventually you'll have to give that up. You can't carry my baby if you're always high."

"Carry your baby?"

"Yes, you don't ever want to have kids?"

"I just never thought you saw me as a woman you'd want to be your baby's mother."

"I don't. I see you as a woman who would be my wife and the mother of my children."'

"Really?" she didn't seem convinced.

"Yes. You're the only woman I can see myself spending the rest of my life with."

"Are you going to answer me?!" Elesia's shouting shook Damacio out of reminiscing over the past.

"What was the question?" he asked, noticing his phone vibrating on the nightstand.

"Are you serious? I'm trying to discuss marriage and babies with you, and you're flaking out on me!" she griped, tossing the hand-woven alpaca wool throw pillow at Damacio.

"I'll be back. I need to take this call," he told Elesia, tossing the pillow back on the bed.

"This conversation is not over!" she yelled, tossing every pillow she could get ahold of at the door as Damacio walked out and closed it. Elesia was incensed. Her ego didn't want to admit that not only was Damacio not interested in babies and marriage with her, but he was also still in love with his wife. She never shied away from a little competition but only when she was confident, she would win. This felt different. Damacio's feelings for his wife ran deep and Elesia didn't want to be any man's consolation prize.

Although she was exaggerating about wanting to have a baby immediately, Elesia was telling no lies when she stated she couldn't prance around in her panties forever. Being a lingerie model had been very beneficial for the curvy beauty. It was the prime reason she had dated countless rich men. But after five years of posing in front of the camera in her undies and being in her late twenties, she knew the clock was ticking. It was time for her to lock down one of these wealthy men and become a rich man's wife. Elesia would love for it to be Damacio, he had the money, looks and the sex was amazing. But Elesia was no fool. She decided right there in the bed, that if Damacio did not sign his divorce papers by the end of the month, she was packing her shit and moving on. Elesia planned on cashing in on her beauty while she was still in demand.

Chapter Fifteen

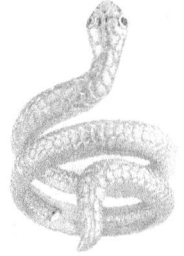

Wants and Needs

Allen Collins sat on the circular couch in the upper deck sky lounge of his Quantum of Solace motor yacht, that was docked at a private marina outside of Houston. It was surrounded by 2,500 acres of expansive Hill Country with 4,070 feet of private waterfront. There were endless amenities available exclusively to owners and their guests, including a covered indoor garden with an 82-foot indoor pool, spa, private restaurant, indoor athletic and wellness center with an indoor clay tennis court, 98- seat theater, and 400- foot infinity edge pool.

It was a safe haven for Allen to escape when he needed to strategize in his personal and professional life.

"Boss, I just got off the phone with one of my guys and still no luck locating Chi or Delancey," Jackson informed him after coming upstairs from the main deck.

"Damn, I hate our men didn't kill them when they had the chance." Allen slammed his hand down on the large marble countertop. He made it a priority when making legal and illegal moves not to leave aspects or elements unresolved or unfinished. "Having loose ends is never good."

"I get that, but I don't think you have anything to worry about." Jackson tried to put his boss at ease. "Once they knew Ashton had been rescued, I'm sure they got the hell out of town and didn't look back. Delancey knew he was guaranteed to die once you found out he tried to rape your daughter."

"The problem is somebody is talking, because that sonofabitch Caesar came to my home and told me he knew it was me who had Ashton kidnapped."

"That man could just be talking. Remember, after you had me look into him, I found out that he was Alejo's replacement for you. Since Alejo has Caesar moving his product in Houston, what if he had him come see you and make that accusation. You know in an attempt to see if you would take the bait and incriminate yourself," Jackson theorized. "You know how messy Alejo can be. Besides, I'm sure he's willing to do just about anything to clear his name."

"Maybe, that could be a possibility, but this is too consequential to be making guesses. And what about Caesar? He is problematic," Allen heaved.

"That's another no, boss," Jackson shook his head. "I hate I have to keep telling you no one has been able to deliver, but I know you prefer the truth. Caesar is extremely lowkey and is proving difficult to locate. One of the partners in his organization being kidnapped and killed, I'm sure also has him on high alert. He's probably being very cautious with the moves he makes."

"Yet another loose end. I need you to do better, Jackson. There's a lot on the line. The only positive outcome you've brought to me in the last few months is getting rid of Crystal. But I need more, specifically, Caesar. If we can get rid of him then I believe everything else will work itself out."

"Boss, I got you. We always figure shit out and get things done, this is no different. The same way I got rid of Crystal, I will get rid of Caesar," Jackson pledged.

"Jackson, you know I always say watch your thoughts, they become words. Watch your words, they become actions. Watch your actions, they become habits. Watch your habits, they become character. Watch your character, it becomes your destiny. So, I'm banking on you keeping your word, because the outcome will determine my destiny."

"I've been working with you for many years now and I understand the value of loyalty, which is why I can appreciate the cost of betrayal. I know where you started and how far you've come. So, I will make sure I do everything within my power to guarantee that your destiny reflects your greatness."

"I know you will. You've consistently shown your allegiance, so I've never had a reason to doubt your devotion. I'm having this conversation with you because I need you to fully understand how crucial this moment is. I've done my share of dirt but the motivation behind my decisions were always based on protecting my wife and kids. There is a legacy I want to leave for my family, and nobody needs to know how deep down in the mud I went to make that happen," Allen emphasized.

"Message received. Your legacy will be protected at all costs. I promise." Jackson and Allen shook hands solidifying their allegiance to the cause.

"Vannette hi," Ashton said, after hitting accept on her iPhone.

"Did I catch you at a bad time?"

"Not at all. How are you?"

"I'm good, I was calling to check on you. We haven't spoken since you left me and Lizzie at the restaurant. How is everyone doing, especially Clayton?"

"As you can imagine horrible. My mother is making the arrangements for Brianna's funeral because Clayton is understandably distraught. I've never seen my brother like this before. I feel guilty for ever thinking he had ice running through his veins. I'm not used to seeing him vulnerable."

"He did lose a child. That has to be devastating. Is he staying at the house with you all?"

"No. My mother tried to get him to, but he wants to stay at his townhouse. He doesn't want to step foot in that beautiful house he recently closed on. He already put it back on the market," Ashton revealed.

"Are you serious…why?"

"I guess because his fiancé got murdered there." Ashton stated dryly. "I mean can you blame him."

"Of course not," Vannette forced herself to agree. Although she was furious. She visualized herself moving into the house and decorating it after helping Clayton mourn the loss of his unborn child. She felt a sense of betrayal that he had made the decision to put it up for sale without consulting her.

"Let me call you back a little later. I just pulled up to Damacio's club."

"Oh wow, is there a reconciliation in the works?"

"No. That ship has sailed. We're discussing a few things regarding the divorce before he signs the papers."

"I'm sorry, Ashton. I know you're with Zephan now, but there has to be a sense of sadness finalizing your divorce."

"There is but we've both moved on. I'm just ready to put this behind me. The sooner the better."

"I understand. I'll let you go handle your business

but call me later. I'm always here if you need me."

"Thanks so much Vannette and ditto. I'll call you later."

When Vannette hung up with Ashton, she started to call Clayton but stopped herself. What she had to say to him couldn't be done over the phone, and decided it was time to give her condolences to her former lover in person.

Ashton had to stop for a second before opening the door to go inside Damacio's club. She was overcome with that nervous, queasy feeling in her stomach. She swallowed hard, took a deep breath and entered the building. There was a young woman sitting at the bar who appeared to be going through some receipts.

"Can I help you?" she asked looking up.

"Yes, I'm here to see Damacio."

"Do you have an appointment?"

"Ashton, hello," Damacio said coming from around the back. "This is my assistant Hailey. Hailey this is my wife, Ashton."

"I'm so sorry," Hailey uttered, seeming to feel completely embarrassed.

"It's totally okay. It's not like I've been a present wife," Ashton remarked coyly.

"Well, now you both have been introduced, so there won't be any confusion. Ashton, how about we talk in my office."

"Sure, and Hailey it was a pleasure meeting you," Ashton smiled.

"You too."

"You look beautiful, Ashton," Damacio commented when they got to his office.

"Thank you but is there a reason you sound surprised by my appearance?"

"If I was going to be honest…"

"I wouldn't expect anything else from you," Ashton cut Damacio off and said.

"As your drug use became more frequent it began to affect the way you looked. You were still beautiful but that spark in your eyes began to dim. Now that spark is back and it's brighter than ever. My point is you look extremely healthy. Rehab was definitely the right decision for you."

"Thank you," Ashton smiled, as the dreaded stomach in knots consumed her. Even now, Damacio still had this effect on her, where she would become flustered and aroused, but she was determined to fight it.

"Are you back in Houston permanently, or are you going back to rehab in California?"

"I'm still in rehab but I'm doing an outpatient treatment here in Houston. I've made a lot of progress with my treatment, and they felt I was ready," Ashton said, fidgeting with one of the buttons on the embellished black blazer she was wearing. "How's everything going with you and your nightclubs?"

"Great. Houston has a very lucrative nightlife.

Right now, it's the daytime, all is quiet and relaxed but, in a few hours, there will be a line down the street and this place will be full to capacity."

"I'm not surprised. The club scene was always your thing."

"Yeah, I'm having a grand opening for a new club in a couple months. Maybe you can come."

"Is that an invite?"

"An invite to what?" Elesia entered Damacio's office interrupting the couple's attempt at fourplay through casual communication.

"Elesia hi, I wasn't aware you were stopping by here today," Damacio said, hoping this wasn't about to turn uncomfortable.

"I didn't know I needed a reason to stop by and visit my boyfriend at his club," she quipped to Damacio, then turning her attention to the familiar looking woman. "I'm Elesia and you must be Ashton."

"Yes, I am. For some reason I feel like I met you before."

"Oh, yes at the house a few months ago."

"That's right, you came out our bedroom naked, but I guess it's your bedroom now."

"I don't know if I would say that."

"Elesia, can you excuse us for a little bit. I need to discuss a few things with Ashton before she has to go."

"Sure, I'll give you both some privacy."

"She's territorial much," Ashton snarked, when Elesia left out the office. "But I think that might be a trait you like in your women because I used to be that way about you too," Ashton laughed, thinking about the time she was ready to drag a woman for sitting too close to Damacio. "Enough about that, do you have those signed divorce papers for me?"

"I do have them," Damacio said grabbing the papers from his desk and holding them up. "But I haven't signed them yet. I had a couple questions I wanted to ask you first."

"Okay, what kind of questions?"

"I know we weren't married very long but you're entitled to spousal support. I don't have a problem providing you with that for the next year or two. Especially if you don't want to move back home with your parents and prefer to get your own place."

"Damacio that is extremely considerate of you to offer. Especially since I definitely wasn't the best wife. But umm, I don't need any spousal support."

"Does that mean you're moving back home?"

"I am staying with my parents right now, but I do plan on moving in with my boyfriend at some point."

"That would be the rapper guy," Damacio said dismissively, not wanting him to seem important.

"Yes, Zephan."

"Were you in rehab with him?"

"I was."

"Do they recommend patients who meet at rehab to become romantically involved?"

"I don't think it matters either way."

"Having two recovering addicts become romantically involved in a serious relationship, seems somewhat dangerous."

"I'll be fine," Ashton snapped becoming defensive.

"He lives the lifestyle of a rapper. I'm positive he's around drugs and alcohol all the time. Which means temptation will constantly surround you."

"You're a club owner. Nothing but drugs and alcohol are around you too," she countered.

"True, but we both know I don't use drugs and never have. So, I'm not battling those temptations on a daily basis. You nor your rapper boyfriend can say the same thing."

"You can stop talking down on me, Damacio. And I'm not your problem anymore. You stopped making me your problem a long time ago. And for clarification, Zephan isn't my boyfriend, he's, my fiancé. Since we're being completely honest, I felt I should correct you on that," Ashton retorted.

"Your fiancé. You're planning on getting married so soon after we divorce? You don't feel the need to wait."

"Oh, you mean how you waited to move another woman into our house and in our bed. That sort of wait…because you didn't wait at all," she fumed, ready to punch her soon to be ex-husband in the mouth. "There's someplace I need to be, so can you please give me the divorce papers so I can go."

"I need to have my lawyer look over the papers before I sign them. You know for legal purposes," Damacio said coming from behind his desk. "Once I feel comfortable with everything, I'll sign them and have them sent over to your attorney."

"Fine. I'm not going to argue with you about this. Just let me know when you get it done."

Elesia was sitting at a corner booth near Damacio's office sipping on a glass of wine when she saw Ashton storm out. She did not look like a happy woman, and figured it was because Damacio signed the divorce papers, and she was regretting letting a man like him go. Elesia finished the remainder of her drink and rushed to his office.

"Hi. I just saw Ashton leave. How did everything go?" Elesia walked over and kissed Damacio and then took a seat near his desk.

"Everything went fine."

"You all were able to iron out whatever issues needed to be resolved?"

"For the most part," Damacio huffed, trying to deescalate his frustration over his conversation with Ashton.

"What the fuck is this?!" Elesisa's keen eyes noticed those loathsome divorce papers were still hovering on Damacio's desk. "Please tell me this is your signed copy," she cracked, grabbing the papers.

"I didn't have an opportunity to sign them yet."

"What bogus excuse do you have for not signing the divorce papers?"

"There is no excuse. I'm going to sign them. I'm

hungry. Do you want to go have some lunch?" he asked, not wanting to discuss his pending divorce with Elesia.

"Here I thought, when I saw your wife rushing out your office with anger on her face, it was because you had signed the divorce papers and she was regretting letting you go. Come to find out, her anger is because you keep holding up the fuckin' process. You're still in love with her, aren't you?" she wanted an answer.

"I'm not having this conversation with you, Elesia. Are you coming with me to get something to eat or not?"

"I think it's best you eat alone." Elesia stood up and grabbed her purse. "You're an amazing man and if you were my husband, I would not let you go but you're the one that's having a hard time letting go. I don't do well being any man's filler, while he pines away over another woman. I'm moving out and moving on with my life. I don't typically give advice on love, especially to men I'm romantically involved with, but I'll make an exception for you. If you still love your wife as much as I think, then put your pride aside and fight for your marriage."

Damacio felt a sense of contentment knowing Elesia was distancing herself from their relationship. Initially their sexual encounter was a way to retaliate against Ashton because he was furious with her drug use and partying ways. But what was supposed to be a short fling became permanent when Ashton left for rehab. So, Elesia ending the relationship now was for the best, because eventually it would've ended regardless. But now that Damacio would no longer be able to use

Elesia as a distraction, he couldn't deny that he was still in love with Ashton. He wanted his wife back, but between Ashton believing his father was responsible for her kidnapping, and now being in a serious relationship with another man, Damacio was no longer sure he could salvage their marriage, but he was determined to try.

Chapter Sixteen

Possessive Love

"Damacio, why are you calling me? We said everything we needed to say to one another the other day."

"I thought we had but I need to see you."

"I don't think that's a good idea."

"I wanted to bring you the divorce papers. I signed them."

"You did?" Ashton was taken aback by Damacio's announcement. "Why the sudden change? I thought you wanted to have your attorney look them over."

"That was an excuse. I have an issue with you getting engaged to Zephan and I don't think you should marry him, but I realize I have to respect your decision, so I won't stand in your way."

"Thank you for not fighting me. I appreciate that."

"So, can I stop by and bring you the signed papers? I would like to hand them to you in person because I do want to talk to you about something."

"I actually have plans for this evening and..."

"It won't take long. I promise," Damacio said hearing the hesitation in his soon to be ex-wife's voice.

"Sure," Ashton reluctantly agreed. "I'll see you when you get here."

Ashton laid down on her bed and stared up at the Niagara chandelier. She tended to do that often, when she wanted to get lost in her thoughts. Her mind drifted as she gazed at the handmade fairies on the elaborate light fixture that was created with fiber optic technology to produce subtle points of light that fall in cascade. It was enriched with golden luster, creating the perfect luminosity in Ashton's bedroom. But instead of the calming effect the chandelier typically had, Ashton found herself tossing and turning in her bed. She wasn't sure if it was because she was about to walk down the aisle again, so soon after one failed marriage. Or was it because her heart still belonged to Damacio. She was torn, but now that her soon to be ex-husband would be bringing over the signed divorce papers, it no longer mattered.

"Vannette, what are you doing here?" Clayton's typical clean-cut persona seemed to be a thing of the past. He hadn't shaved or gotten a haircut. His eyes were squinting when he opened the door as if the sun had become his enemy. The lack of sleep was also evident from the dark circles beneath his typical alert and vibrant eyes.

"I wanted to check on you," Vannette said, leaning in and kissing Clayton on his cheek. "I also brought some of your favorites from that deli around the corner from your office building. Why don't you let me come in. I can tidy things up," she volunteered, noticing how cluttered and disorganized his townhouse was.

"Sure, come on in." Clayton left the door ajar and walked off to sit back down on the couch to watch television. This had become his norm for the past week. "What are you doing?"

"Just opening the blinds, so you can get some much-needed sunlight in here."

"I don't want any sunlight. Close that shit back up," he barked.

"Clayton, I know you're in a bad place right now, but things will get better. In the meantime, you need to take care of yourself. Being hauled up in a dark room won't help you heal." Vannette spoke lovingly thinking she could reach him.

"Don't tell me what the fuck I need to do. How would you know. You haven't loss anything."

"That's not true. I loss our baby, remember. That miscarriage was devastating to me."

"Whatever." Clayton threw up his hand. "At some point you can always get pregnant again. I can't get back Brianna and our child," he stated scornfully.

"I did consider that, and I'm glad you want me to get pregnant again too because I want us to start a family together," Vannette said filled with optimism.

"What are you talking about? I don't want to start a family with you. I meant you can have a baby with somebody else, not with me," he voiced callously.

"But Brianna is gone now. You don't have to choose between us, so now we can be together."

"Are you high? No, I'm serious." Clayton sat up on the couch and glanced over at Vannette. "I made my choice, I wanted to be with Brianna. Now that some fuckin' monster has killed her and our child, doesn't mean I want you because I don't," he said bluntly.

"You don't mean that Clayton," Vannette shook her head in denial. "Right now, you're hurt because you lost your child."

"And the woman that I love!" he quickly added.

"You don't love Brianna."

"Yes, the fuck I do. Why the hell do you think I was going to marry her."

"For the baby. Once I had a miscarriage, you felt obligated to marry her. It had nothing to do with love."

"Yo, your fuckin' crazy. I don't know where this shit is coming from. When I first found out you were pregnant, I considered marrying you, out of a sense of obligation. But Brianna never put any pressure on me or made me feel obligated. I was in love with her, and I wanted us to raise our child together. Now, that's been ripped away from me, and I don't know if I'll ever get over it." Clayton put his head down, wishing he could make his heartache go away.

"I can't believe you were actually in love with that scandalous bitch!" Vannette screamed. "I would've done anything for you, but you preferred her over me."

"Yo, get the fuck out my house," Clayton stood up and said. "I should've never let your crazy ass in."

"You're right, you shouldn't have. I can't believe I thought you ever loved me," Vannette cried.

"Love you...you're too pathetic to love." Clayton waved Vannette off, walking towards the door to get her out his house. His cavalier attitude left him defenseless against the woman who went from being a lovesick puppy to a psychotic killer.

"All I ever wanted was for you to love me," Vannette purged her heart, before pumping two bullets to the back of Clayton's head, then turning the gun on herself.

Chapter Seventeen

Into The Darkness

"Thank you for seeing me," Damacio said when Ashton opened the door.

"It's not a problem," she said letting him inside. "When we saw each other the other day, it ended badly. I don't want there to be animosity between us."

"I agree. Just because our marriage is coming to an end, doesn't mean we can't be friends." Damacio stated following Ashton into the living room.

"Can I get you something to drink," she offered.

"Sure, I'll have some water. Is okay if I use the restroom?" he asked glancing around the room.

"Of course. It's down the hall," Ashton pointed in the direction of the bathroom, before heading towards the kitchen, when she ran into her parents. "Hey! I didn't realize you all were still home."

"Yes. We just finished having lunch," Karmen told Ashton.

"It was more like a picnic. I wanted to do something romantic for your mother," Allen said, placing his arm around his wife's waist.

"And it was. Your father had this very elaborate meal for us on the terrace overlooking the pond and formal garden. It was sweet and beautiful," Karmen gushed, kissing her husband.

"Wow, it's really wonderful seeing my parents like this, so in love." Ashton hugged them tightly.

"Yes, it's like old times only better. Our love is stronger than ever," Allen remarked proudly.

"I don't want to disturb all this love flowing in the air, but I wanted to let you know that Damacio is here."

"What is he doing here?"

"Dad, he just came over to drop off the signed divorce papers and he wanted to talk. I didn't think anyone was home. If I knew you were going to be here, I wouldn't have let him come."

"You don't have to explain yourself Ashton. This is your home too and it's fine that Damacio is here," Karmen reassured her daughter. "Your father can be cordial to Damacio, right Allen?"

"Yes," he exhaled.

"Thank you both so much. I'm headed to the kitchen to get Damacio some water. He went to the restroom but I'm sure he's back in the living room now, so be nice, dad," Ashton smiled.

"He will be," her mother promised.

"The only reason I agreed to be cordial to that imbecile is because I know our daughter will soon be rid of him."

"Allen, no matter what you think of Damacio, Ashton was very much in love with him and even if she won't admit it, this divorce has to be difficult for her."

"Ashton is a smart young lady and much stronger than you think. She's already moving on from Damacio. Albeit a fuckin' rapper, but anything is better than the son of Alejo."

"Allen, please..." Karmen couldn't finish her sentence as she was stunned into silence when they entered the living room.

"This is very convenient. We were planning on sharing this information with just Ashton, now we can share it with you also, Karmen. Since you already know what this is about, there is no need for you to be here, but you're more than welcome to have a seat and listen," Caesar mocked.

"Muthafucka, you better get the hell out my house because this time you won't be walking out, you'll be carried out," Allen threatened.

"Caesar, how did you even get in here?" Karmen

wanted to know.

"I let him in," Damacio spoke up and said.

"You got my daughter to let you in my home and then you bring in this trash with you. You disloyal piece of shit. But I wouldn't expect anything less from Alejo's son," Allen fumed.

"Caesar, you need to leave. You have no business being here. Please leave," Karmen insisted.

"I can't do that. Ashton deserves to know the truth," Caesar pushed back, determined to make sure the patriarch of the Collins family had to answer for his treachery.

"The truth about what?" Ashton was confused as to what she walked in on. "Wait, aren't you the man who saved my life that night at Damacio's club?" she recalled.

Allen stepped off to the side and called Jackson while Ashton was speaking with Caesar.

"Hey boss, what can I do for you?"

"I need you to get over here immediately and bring backup. How far away are you?"

"Not far at all. We were on our way to the warehouse to prepare for tomorrows shipment. We'll head to you instead."

"Yes, come now. Damacio and Caesar are here. Things are getting ugly, so come prepared to shoot and kill them the moment you arrive."

"Daddy, what is Caesar talking about? He said he knows who was responsible for my kidnapping and it wasn't Alejo."

"Both of you!" Allen pointed his finger at Damacio and Caesar, "Need to get the hell out my house!"

"My wife deserves to know the truth about what you did to her. That it wasn't my father who had her kidnapped but you!" Damacio exploded, charging across the room towards Allen.

"Please stop!" Ashton stood in front of Damacio, determined to maintain distance between her husband and father.

"Allen, what is Damacio talking about?" Karmen stared at her husband with confusion and disbelief.

"Nothing but lies. These two pieces of shit are clearly trying to destroy our family and creating malicious lies to do so," Allen said, doing his best to convince his wife he was telling the truth.

"Kasir, thank God you're here," Ashton said, desperately wanting backup to help keep the peace.

"What is going on in here, and who are you?" Kasir questioned staring over at Caesar, but he didn't respond, Karmen did.

"Kasir, that's Caesar. He's here by way of Damacio," Karmen explained.

"And he has made a horrible accusation about our father!" Ashton shouted, turning to Damacio. "I understand you don't want to believe your father had anything to do with my kidnapping, but to accuse my father is beyond disgusting."

"Wait, you're saying our father is the reason Ashton was kidnapped?" Kasir repeated the question making sure he was receiving the information accurately.

"Nothing but lies, son," Allen said denying the claim.

"Of course, it's lies. My father would never do that to me! That kidnapping was the worst experience of my life. How dare you blame my father!" Ashton wailed.

"Dad, did you have anything to do with Ashton's kidnapping?" Kasir asked flatly.

"How can you even ask me a question like that." Allen sounded offended.

"Because you're the reason Crystal is dead."

"Crystal is dead?" Karmen glanced over at her husband blindsided by the revelation.

"Who is Crystal?" Ashton had never heard the name before.

"It was a woman that I was seeing. But I found out before we had become involved, she had been having an affair with our father," Kasir told a rattled Ashton.

"You cheated on mom...how could you?"

"Ashton, it was a mistake, and your mother forgave me."

"The point is Ashton; our father is capable of doing a lot of things in order to get what he wants. He had Jackson shoot Crystal because he saw her as a liability. She was in a coma for weeks, finally succumbing to her injuries. Before she died, she wanted me to know that my father was responsible for her death and to get her justice."

"That's enough, Kasir!" Allen roared.

"Allen, tell me these are all lies," Karmen implored.

"Of course, it is! Tell me you don't believe these vicious lies!"

"Why don't we ask the men you hired to kidnap your own daughter," Caesar said, having his shooters bring out Chi and Delancey, who'd been stashed in a back room since Damacio first let them in.

Ashton immediately began shaking when she laid eyes on the man who tried to rape her. Seeing him bound and gagged did little to ease her anxiety.

"Baby, it's okay." Damacio wrapped his arms around Ashton, holding her close. "He can't hurt you. I'm sorry I wasn't there to protect you, but nobody will ever hurt you again," he vowed.

"Tell us who hired you to kidnap Ashton? Caesar directed, having one of his shooters rip the tape off Chi's mouth.

"I was hired by Allen Collins," Chi announced.

"I've never seen that man in my life!" Allen refuted.

"I didn't get the money from that man, I got it from him," Chi said nodding his head towards Jackson, who just entered the room. Before any other words could be exchanged, Jackson and his men followed orders and began shooting to kill.

With a detrimental stare at the intended targets, Jackson pulled the trigger first, setting off a chain reaction of blistering combat within the confines of the modern Tudor showplace at their River Oaks estate. Jackson and his men were met with fierce resistance by Caesar's shooters. The rapid gunfire had everyone in the midst of warfare, fleeing for their lives and taking cover.

As swiftly as the gunfire erupted, it can to an abrupt and ominous end. Ashton felt the heaviness of Damacio's body on top of her, as he acted as her shield. She was afraid to call out his name, fearing he might be dead. But when she felt a slight movement, it gave her the courage to speak.

"Damacio, are you okay?" she questioned trying to lift his body and that's when she felt this wetness on her hand, realizing it was blood. "Oh God, please don't be dead."

"I'm not dead," Damacio assured Ashton, pealing his body off her.

"You're bleeding."

"I'm okay. I was shot in my arm. What about you, are you okay?"

"I'm fine because you protected me."

"I promised you that no one would ever hurt you again, and I meant it."

"Thank you, but we still need to get your armed looked at. But Thank God we're okay, what about everyone else?" Ashton wondered, as both she and Damacio stood up to skim over the room. It was eerily quiet, and they weren't sure who was dead and who was alive. Then they were left alarmed by a sudden outburst.

"NOOOOOOOOOOOO!!" was the gut-wrenching scream Ashton heard before her world seemed to go pitch black.

Epilogue ...

A heartbroken wife and mother, Karmen Collins, read from Scriptures in a church fragrant with roses and orchids. She stood stoic in a body-skimming silhouette dress with floral applique, square neckline, scallop cuffs and hems with Italian-style guipure lace on the long sleeves and bodice. After the eulogy, the choir belted out a passionate rendition of the gospel song, More Than I Can Bear. Prominent Houston business leaders and local politicians were amongst the 500 mourners who came to pay their last respects at the joint funeral service for Allen and Clayton Collins. Both men lay in open mahogany coffins, each wearing Desmond Merrion hand stitched suits. Once the service ended, a procession of more than a dozen stretch limousines joined two flower cars, a horse-drawn carriage, and the hearses carrying the bodies of father and son.

"That was a beautiful service," Ashton said, holding her mother's hand.

"I think your father and brother would've been pleased." Karmen gave a guarded smile, hiding her sorrow beneath the oversized black squared sunglasses.

"Yes, although I still can't believe they're both dead. Clayton shot and killed by someone I considered a close friend, who then killed herself and was responsible for killing Brianna too. I can't even wrap my head around Vannette being capable of such heinous murders. And then dad," Ashton stopped herself, because she instantly got choked up. She was always a daddy's girl and losing her father was devastating.

"I know how traumatic this is for you Ashton, but I promise we will get through it."

"Honestly, at first, I thought I was going to relapse. The pain was overbearing, but Damacio has been amazing. The only blessing that came out of this tragedy is my marriage was saved. Our bond is unbreakable, and I realize I love my husband more than anything."

"That is a blessing, because Damacio truly does love you."

"There is one other good thing that came out of this," Ashton added.

"And what's that?" Karmen turned to her daughter and asked.

"We found out the truth. Daddy had nothing to do with my kidnapping or that woman Crystal's murder. It was all Jackson. He went rogue. Making horrible decisions he knew our father would never approve of. Then firing the shot that ended his life. I still wonder if he killed our father on purpose."

"Don't put any energy into wondering about that because we'll probably never know the truth, and it doesn't even matter," Karmen reasoned, staring out the window during the limousine ride to the private graveside service that was only for immediate family members.

"You're right, it doesn't matter because Jackson is in prison where he belongs. We will continue to celebrate and honor our father for the great man that he was." Ashton stated without wavering.

"You are correct," Karmen nodded, as they waited for the driver to open the door. When she stepped out the limo, she noticed a familiar face walking towards her.

"Mom, isn't that Caesar coming this way?" Ashton asked.

"Yes, that is him."

"First, he saved my life at the nightclub, and then he saved your life when all those bullets rang out at our house. If it wasn't for him, I would've lost you and dad that day. I will always be grateful to him. Hi Caesar, it's good to see you." Ashton gave him a warm embrace.

"It's good to see you too, although I wish it was under different circumstances. Do you mind if I speak with your mother for a moment?"

"Of course not. Mom, I'll be over there with Kasir."

"Okay, I'll join you shortly," Karmen told her daughter. She waited to say anything further until Ashton was unable to hear her conversation with Caesar.

"I know you didn't want me to come but I needed to see you."

"It's too soon, Caesar. We haven't even buried my husband yet."

"I get that but how long are you going to play the grieving wife role?"

"What do you mean, I am grieving. I lost my youngest son and my husband."

"I understand grieving your son, but you know the truth about your husband. I still don't understand why you feel the need to protect him."

"Is that what you think I'm doing, protecting my husband?"

"Isn't it?" Caesar's expression showed his disapproval.

"No, I'm protecting my family, which means preserving my husband's legacy. There is no need for my children and everyone else to know what a monster he was. Allen is dead, the men responsible for kidnapping and trying to rape Ashton are dead, and Jackson is in prison. I believe justice has been served."

"You don't think Jackson might one day want to tell the full story, and let everyone know that he didn't act alone but was following the orders of his boss?"

"No. Jackson has always been resolute with his loyalty to Allen. He voluntarily made a confession taking full responsibly for Ashton's kidnapping and Crystal's murder. That book has been officially closed. I will now do my part to guarantee our family's name is respected and Kasir is able to continue building upon the legacy his father started."

"I respect that. But what about us? I'm still very much in love with you Karmen. If I could, I would get down on bended knee right now and ask you to be my wife, but I know that's not what you want from me right now."

"You're right, it's not but I am still in love with you too. I can't ask you to wait for me, but when the time is right, I do want us to be together. I have to go. They're waiting on me to start the service. Goodbye, Caesar."

As Karmen walked away, she could feel his loving gaze.

"Not goodbye but until, because I will wait for you until the end of time," Karmen heard Caesar say, filling her heart with joy.

The End

A KING PRODUCTION

PLATINUM EDITION

Bitch

Precious Cummings Is Back...

A Novel

Joy Deja King

A KING PRODUCTION

Deadly Divorce...

A Titillating Tale

Toxic Series

A Novelette

JOY DEJA KING

Chapter One

Banking On Me

"What do you mean I didn't get the part?" Londyn swallowed hard. "You said the casting director loved me."

"Chris does," her agent Misty confirmed.

"Then what happened?!" Londyn's tone was loud and hostile, causing people in the restaurant to turnaround and briefly stare. She took a deep breath and lowered her voice. "When I got the callback and auditioned for the casting director and director, they both seemed extremely pleased with my audition. You even said I was a shoo-in for the role, so what happened?"

"You know I'm always transparent with you," Misty sighed. "Well, as you're aware the production is a big budget film and is supposed to be on track for box office gold."

"Exactly! This role was finally going to get me off the B-list and make me an A-list superstar."

"And you know I want that for you. You deserve it, and I still believe it will happen," she added.

"Stop bullshitting me and tell me why I didn't get the part," Londyn fumed.

"Supposedly, they're saying the producer requested a specific actress to be attached to the production who has the ability to fill up the movie theater. But off the record, Chris confided in me that the producer went over his head and the director, pulled some strings, and got the actress he wanted," Misty explained.

"Who is she?"

Misty hesitated for a moment. "Veronica Woods...I know I know," she put her hands up and said, knowing what Londyn was going to say next.

"Veronica! She can't fill up an elementary school play let alone a movie theater," Londyn seethed. "She's barely C-list!"

"Listen, everything you're saying, I said it and more with expletives. I'm being calm now, but I was livid. Chris finally admitted to me that whoever Veronica is dating, the producer owes him a huge favor and he called it in."

"So, Veronica got the part that I busted my ass off for, because of who she's fuckin'." Londyn rolled her eyes looking completely defeated.

"We both know this industry can be cruel and there's nothing fair about it. I hate seeing this disappointment on your face, but we'll push through like we always do," Misty said placing her hand on Londyn's arm.

"I just knew it was finally my time," Londyn's voice trailed off, she said shaking her head.

"Chris really is a fan of yours. He thought you were perfect for the lead but because of the Veronica situation, he offered you another part. Of course, it's a much smaller role but it will give you an opportunity to be seen by millions of people."

"I don't think I'm interested in his consolation prize."

"Londyn, don't look at it that way. View it as an opportunity to shine. This could lead to a bigger role in another movie."

"How many times have I heard that." Londyn's attitude had become cynical. "I'm not eighteen, just getting off the bus. I've been doing this for over ten years, and I feel like I've been stuck. My career seems to have reached a plateau. I'll never be a bankable actress."

"That's not necessarily true. Lots of talented and beautiful actresses don't reach superstar status until much later in their career," Misty said with optimism in her voice. From the dismal expression on Londyn's face, she could see her words of encouragement weren't working. "Just consider taking the other role Chris is offering you. And don't forget, ABC really wants you for their new crime drama."

"I'm not interested in doing a television show, plus the networks are saturated with crime dramas. The show will probably be cancelled after the first season," Londyn complained.

"Will you at least consider the smaller role Chris is offering...please," Misty pleaded.

"Sure, I'll think about it," Londyn exhaled, standing up. "But I have to go. I don't want to be late for Ryan's first major exhibit at that art gallery tonight, so I need to get to my hair appointment," she said grabbing her purse.

"That's right, Ryan's exhibit is tonight. Let him know I never received my invite."

"I told you he said that was an oversight and you are most definitely invited. He'll be disappointed if you don't show up."

"I highly doubt that, but if you insist, I guess I can come," Misty smirked. "Besides, I heard it's the place to be tonight. Ryan must be elated."

"More like thankful he is finally getting the recognition he deserves. Ryan has always had a vision and stayed focused. It's going to be amazing to see his vision come to life." Londyn smiled proudly at how far her friend had come, and the direction his career was heading in.

"A minute ago I was worried the frown on your face was permanent but now that winning smile is back. I'll have to thank Ryan when I see him tonight."

"Yeah, I'll have to thank him too. He inspires me. We both got to LA around the same time. After all the time and work he's put in at the studio, Ryan has finally gotten his big breakthrough. Maybe that means my big break is coming too," Londyn winked.

Misty desperately wanted the same thing for Londyn. She still remembered the day Londyn walked into her office begging for representation. She read a feature Variety Magazine had recently done on Misty and was adamant she was the only agent for her. She was so full of passion yet extremely stubborn, refusing to take no for an answer. That was the main reason Misty couldn't deny her request, although she was a complete unknown. Londyn soon became her favorite client. She had this sparkle and tenacity in her eyes that made you root for her. She still had that same spark, but Misty was afraid that if Londyn didn't reach the success she desired, that fire would soon burn out.

A KING PRODUCTION

Rich or Famous

Rich Because You Can Buy Fame

A NOVEL

JOY DEJA KING

Lorenzo
Welcome To My World
★ ★★★ ★

Before I die, if you don't remember anything else I ever taught you, know this. A man will be judged, not on what he has but how much of it. So you find a way to make money and when you think you've made enough, make some more, because you'll need it to survive in this cruel world. Money will be the only thing to save you. As I sat across from Darnell those words my father said to me on his deathbed played in my head.

"Yo, Lorenzo, are you listening to me, did you hear anything I said?"

"I heard everything you said. The problem for you is I don't give a fuck." I responded, giving a casual shoulder shrug as I rested my thumb under my chin with my index finger above my mouth.

"What you mean, you don't give a fuck? We been doing business for over three years now and that's the best you got for me?"

"Here's the thing, Darnell, I got informants all over these streets. As a matter of fact that broad you've had in your back pocket for the last few weeks is one of them."

"I don't understand what you saying," Darnell said swallowing hard. He tried to keep the tone of his voice calm, but his body composure was speaking something different.

"Alexus, has earned every dollar I've paid her to fuck wit' yo' blood suckin' ass. You a fake fuck wit' no fangs. You wanna play wit' my 100 g's like you at the casino. That's a real dummy move, Darnell." I could see the sweat beads gathering, resting in the creases of Darnell's forehead.

"Lorenzo, man, I don't know what that bitch told you but none of it is true! I swear 'bout four niggas ran up in my crib last night and took all my shit. Now that I think about it, that trifling ho Alexus probably had me set up! She fucked us both over!"

I shook my head for a few seconds not believing this muthafucker was saying that shit with a straight face. "I thought you said it was two niggas that ran up in your crib now that shit done doubled. Next thing you gon' spit is that all of Marcy projects was in on the stickup."

"Man, I can get your money. I can have it to you first thing tomorrow. I swear!"

"The thing is I need my money right now." I casually stood up from my seat and walked towards Darnell who now looked like he had been dipped in water. Watching him fall apart in front of my eyes made up for the fact that I would never get back a dime of the money he owed me.

"Zo, you so paid, this shit ain't gon' even faze you. All I'm asking for is less than twenty-four hours. You can at least give me that," Darnell pleaded.

"See, that's your first mistake, counting my pockets. My money is *my* money, so yes this shit do faze me."

"I didn't mean it like that. I wasn't tryna disrespect you. By this time tomorrow you will have your money and we can put this shit behind us." Darnell's eyes darted around in every direction instead of looking directly at me. A good liar, he was not.

"Since you were robbed of the money you owe me and the rest of my drugs, how you gon' get me my dough? I mean the way you tell it, they didn't leave you wit' nothin' but yo' dirty draws."

"I'll work it out. Don't even stress yourself, I got you, man."

"What you saying is that the nigga you so called aligned yourself with, by using my money and my product, is going to hand it back over to you?"

"Zo, what you talking 'bout? I ain't aligned myself wit' nobody. That slaw ass bitch Alexus feeding you lies."

"No, that's you feeding me lies. Why don't you admit you no longer wanted to work for me? You felt you was big shit and could be your own boss. So you used my money and product to buy your way in with this other nigga to step in my territory. But you ain't no boss you a poser. And your need to perpetrate a fraud is going to cost you your life."

"Lorenzo, don't do this man! This is all a big misunderstanding. I swear on my daughter I will have your money tomorrow. Fuck, if you let me leave right now I'll have that shit to you tonight!" I listened to Darnell stutter his words.

My men, who had been patiently waiting in each corner of the warehouse, dressed in all black, loaded with nothing but artillery, stepped out of the darkness ready to obliterate the enemy I had once considered my best worker. Darnell's eyes widened as he witnessed the men who had saved and protected him on numerous occasions, as he dealt with the vultures he encountered in the street life, now ready to end his.

"Don't do this, Zo! Pleeease," Darnell was now on his knees begging.

"Damn, nigga, you already a thief and a backstabber. Don't add, going out crying like a bitch to that too. Man the fuck up. At least take this bullet like a soldier."

"I'm sorry, Zo. Please don't do this. I gotta daughter that need me. Pleeease man, I'll do anything. Just don't kill me." The tears were pouring down Darnell's face and instead of softening me up it just made me even more pissed at his punk ass.

"Save your fuckin' tears. You shoulda thought about your daughter before you stole from me. You're the worse sort of thief. I invite you into my home, I make you a part of my family and you steal from me, you plot against me. Your daughter doesn't need you. You have nothing to teach her."

My men each pulled out their gat ready to attack and I put my hand up motioning them to stop. For the first time since Darnell arrived, a calm gaze spread across his face.

"I knew you didn't have the heart to let them kill me, Zo. We've been through so much together. I mean you Tania's God Father. We bigger than this and we will get through it," Darnell said, halfway smiling as he began getting off his knees and standing up.

"You're right, I don't have the heart to let them kill you, I'ma do that shit myself." Darnell didn't even have a chance to let what I said resonate with him because I just sprayed that muthafucker like the piece of shit he was. "Clean this shit up," I said, stepping over Darnell's bullet ridden body as I made my exit.

A KING PRODUCTION

SUPREME
MEN OF THE BITCH SERIES

JOY DEJA KING

Chapter One

I Will Be King

From my very first recollection as a kid, I remember staring my parents directly in their eyes while sitting at the dinner table and stating without hesitation, "I will be king." I then looked back down at my plate of food and continued to eat.

"Xavier, what did you say?" my mother questioned, seeming completely bewildered by my comment.

"I said, I'll be king," I repeated, shrugging my shoulders in a nonchalant way. Even then at the age of four or five I had this I don't give a fuck aura about myself. When I was younger, people mistook it as me being disengaged from others. When I got older, people labeled me as arrogant, but honestly it was none of the above. I just knew, I always knew, that I would be somebody great, that I would leave a legacy that my children and grandchildren would admire and respect.

"Boy, what are you talking about now?" My dad chuckled, glancing over at my mother. "You always talking crazy. I tell you what you gon' be… a damn comedian." He laughed. My dad didn't mean any harm, he just didn't know any better.

I didn't even respond to my dad. Once again I shrugged my shoulders and continued eating my dinner. At that time, I wasn't sure the path in life I would take that would make me king. I was only sure that greatness awaited me and I was looking forward to taking my spot on the throne.

"Only one more week of school and then summer vacation… yes!" I shouted, pumping my fist in the air.

"It ain't gonna be no vacation for me. I have to go to summer school," my friend, Isaac, complained as we walked home from school.

"I still don't understand how you flunking classes in the 8th grade. I mean we don't even do shit," I said, shaking my head.

"Whatever, Xavier. Everybody can't be a fuckin' genius like you. You don't even have to open a book and already know all the answers. You've always been that way," Isaac huffed, shaking his head.

"You got excuses for everything." I shrugged, quickly losing interest in the conversation because my thirteen-year-old eyes were fixated on the lyrical battle taking place right in front of me. There was a small crowd surrounding the guys who looked to be only a few years older than me. As I walked closer, not only was I able to witness but I could hear them spitting lyrics back and forth to each other. It was a word battle that I had never seen before and the more the verbiage escalated the more intrigued I became.

"Xavier, come on! We need to get home," I heard Isaac call out, but I was paying him no mind. I wanted in on the battle. It was crazy. I had never rapped a lyric a day in my life, but hearing these two young guys who looked just like me, going at it had me mesmerized. Yeah, I had watched rappers on television and heard them on the radio, but being so up close and personal had this profound affect on me.

"Yo, Xavier we need to go!" Isaac yelled, grabbing my arm. "You know I'm on punishment. My moms told me I betta come straight home after school. So let's go or I'ma get in trouble," Isaac complained.

"Man, stop yo' whining. Besides, you on punishment... not me. Take yo' ass home. I'ma stay here and watch this rap battle," I said dropping my book bag. I was ready to make this corner block my home for the rest of the afternoon.

"Yo' you buggin'! I thought you were gon' come to my house and keep me company. My mom said you the only friend I can have over."

"Go 'head." I waved my hand, signaling Isaac to keep it moving. "I'll be over there in a minute."

Isaac glanced at me and then the two guys rapping. "Why you so interested in what they doing?" he questioned, not able to hide his confusion. It was written all over his face.

"'Cause they doing what I'ma do." I nodded my head with confidence.

"And what's that... run yo' mouth? You already know how to do that."

"Nah, dummy!" I shook my head. "I'ma be a rapper."

Isaac fell out laughing. He bent over, dropping his book bag, making this major production like he heard the funniest joke ever. "X, you got mad jokes. So you gon' be on the corner like these two clowns and call yo'self a rapper," he sneered. Isaac was now holding his stomach like he was laughing so hard that he had stomach cramps or something.

"Go 'head… keep laughing." I chuckled. "Wait and see. Not only am I gonna be a rapper. But the streets gon' say I was wanna the best that ever did it. I'ma be a star." Then I paused for a second before continuing. "Fuck a star. I'ma be a superstar." I smiled looking towards the clouds, seeing my vision up in the blue sky."

"Yo, you have officially lost yo' mind," Isaac snorted. "When you get yo' head up outta those clouds, stop by the crib. I'll be waiting on you so we can play some video games."

"Cool." I nodded as Isaac hurried off, but I never made it to his crib that day. I stayed on the block like my shoes were glued to the cement. That afternoon, on a sunny day in Queens, New York, I realized just how I would create my legacy. "Get ready world, 'cause I will be king," I mumbled under my breath as I continued to study the two young men who had become my inspiration.

Read The Entire Bitch Series in This Order

P.O. Box 912
Collierville, TN 38027

A KING PRODUCTION

www.joydejaking.com
www.twitter.com/joydejaking

ORDER FORM

Name:

Address:

City/State:

Zip:

QUANTITY	TITLES	PRICE	TOTAL
	Bitch	$15.00	
	Bitch Reloaded	$15.00	
	The Bitch Is Back	$15.00	
	Queen Bitch	$15.00	
	Last Bitch Standing	$15.00	
	Superstar	$15.00	
	Ride Wit' Me	$12.00	
	Ride Wit' Me Part 2	$15.00	
	Stackin' Paper	$15.00	
	Trife Life To Lavish	$15.00	
	Trife Life To Lavish II	$15.00	
	Stackin' Paper II	$15.00	
	Rich or Famous	$15.00	
	Rich or Famous Part 2	$15.00	
	Rich or Famous Part 3	$15.00	
	Bitch A New Beginning	$15.00	
	Mafia Princess Part 1	$15.00	
	Mafia Princess Part 2	$15.00	
	Mafia Princess Part 3	$15.00	
	Mafia Princess Part 4	$15.00	
	Mafia Princess Part 5	$15.00	
	Boss Bitch	$15.00	
	Baller Bitches Vol. 1	$15.00	
	Baller Bitches Vol. 2	$15.00	
	Baller Bitches Vol. 3	$15.00	
	Bad Bitch	$15.00	
	Still The Baddest Bitch	$15.00	
	Power	$15.00	
	Power Part 2	$15.00	
	Drake	$15.00	
	Drake Part 2	$15.00	
	Female Hustler	$15.00	
	Female Hustler Part 2	$15.00	

QUANTITY	TITLES	PRICE	TOTAL
	Female Hustler Part 3	$15.00	
	Female Hustler Part 4	$15.00	
	Female Hustler Part 5	$15.00	
	Female Hustler Part 6	$15.00	
	Princess Fever "Birthday Bash"	$6.00	
	Nico Carter The Men Of The Bitch Series	$15.00	
	Bitch The Beginning Of The End	$15.00	
	Supreme...Men Of The Bitch Series	$15.00	
	Bitch The Final Chapter	$15.00	
	Stackin' Paper III	$15.00	
	Men Of The Bitch Series And The Women Who Love Them	$15.00	
	Coke Like The 80s	$15.00	
	Baller Bitches The Reunion Vol. 4	$15.00	
	Stackin' Paper IV	$15.00	
	The Legacy	$15.00	
	Lovin' Thy Enemy	$15.00	
	Stackin' Paper V	$15.00	
	The Legacy Part 2	$15.00	
	Assassins - Episode 1	$11.00	
	Assassins - Episode 2	$11.00	
	Assassins - Episode 3	$11.00	
	Bitch Chronicles	$40.00	
	So Hood So Rich	$15.00	
	Stackin' Paper VI	$15.00	
	Female Hustler Part 7	$15.00	
	Toxic...	$11.99	
	Stackin' Paper VII	$15.00	
	Sugar Babies...	$9.99	
	Deadly Divorce...	$11.99	
	The Legacy Part 3	$15.00	

Shipping/Handling (Via Priority Mail) $8.95 1-3 Books, $16.25 4-7 Books. For 7 or more $21.50.
Total: $_____ FORMS OF ACCEPTED PAYMENTS: Certified or government issued checks and money Orders, all mail in orders take 5-7 Business days to be delivered

CPSIA information can be obtained
at www.ICGtesting.com
Printed in the USA
LVHW040342250223
740355LV00001B/129